Nicholas Patrick Wiseman

William Shakespeare

Nicholas Patrick Wiseman

William Shakespeare

ISBN/EAN: 9783337422837

Printed in Europe, USA, Canada, Australia, Japan

Cover: Foto ©Raphael Reischuk / pixelio.de

More available books at **www.hansebooks.com**

WILLIAM SHAKESPEARE.

BY

HIS EMINENCE

CARDINAL WISEMAN.

LONDON:
HURST AND BLACKETT, PUBLISHERS,
SUCCESSORS TO HENRY COLBURN,
13, GREAT MARLBOROUGH STREET.
1865.

PREFACE.

IN the autumn of last year a communication was made to His Eminence the late Cardinal Wiseman by H. Bence Jones, Esq., M.D., as Secretary of the Royal Institution of Great Britain, requesting him to deliver a lecture before that society. The Cardinal, with the prompt kindness usual to him, at once assented. The Shakespeare Tercentenary seemed to prescribe the subject, which His Eminence therefore selected.

The following pages were dictated by him in the last weeks of his life. The latter part was taken down in the beginning of January ; the earlier part was dictated on Saturday the fourteenth of that month. It was his last intellectual exertion, and it overtaxed his failing strength.

The Rev. Dr. Clifford, Chaplain to the Hospital of S. John and S. Elizabeth, who acted as his

amanuensis, states, from the lips of His Eminence,
that the matter contained in these pages is the
beginning and the ending of what he intended
to deliver. We have, therefore, only a fragment
of a whole which was never completed except in
the author's mind. Dr. Clifford adds : "I have
no recollection of the Cardinal's telling me the
manner in which he intended filling up the hiatus,
but the day before his illness he said, 'I shall
have no more real work, for I have every sentence
that I am going to dictate already in my mind ; it
is only a question of time now. I know word for
word what I shall say.' "

It is needless to state that no part of this lecture
has had the benefit of the author's revision. It
may be asked : If then it be no more than a fragment, why publish it? Is it just to the literary
reputation of so great a name ?

The lecture is now published for the following
reasons :

First, because we believe that the beauty of
these pages will abundantly justify their publication. Fragmentary as they are, they are the fragments of such a whole as could hardly come from
any other hand. There is in this lecture an exquisite refinement of thought, and a singular grace-

fulness of intellectual expression, together with a
beauty of outline which it would be difficult to
equal. If the work be imperfect, so, as he tells
us in his opening paragraphs, were the last labours
of others who have gone before him. There is but
one end to the greatest and the noblest minds.
And happy are they who preserve their power,
exuberance, and freshness so vividly even to the
last.

Secondly, this lecture is committed to the press,
because we believe he would have desired us to
give to the people of England the last work he
undertook—even when life and strength were
failing—for their sake. It was his last effort in
their service ; his last endeavour for their rational
pleasure.

Finally, so wide-spread a desire to possess this
lecture has been expressed by His Eminence's
friends, and by many others not personally related
to him, that we do not feel justified in disappointing
a wish which arises from affection and veneration
for his person.

H. E. MANNING.

WILLIAM THOMPSON.

St. Mary's, Bayswater, March, 1865.

WILLIAM SHAKESPEARE.

I.

THERE have been some men in the world's history—and they are necessarily few—who by their deaths have deprived mankind of the power to do justice to their merits, in those particular spheres of excellence in which they had been pre-eminent. When the "immortal" Raphael for the last time laid down his palette, still moist with the brilliant colours which he had spread upon his unfinished masterpiece, destined to be exposed to admiration above his bier, he left none behind him who could worthily depict and transmit to us his beautiful lineaments: so that posterity has had to seek in his own paintings, among the guards at a sepulchre, or among the youthful disciples in an ancient school, some figure which may be considered as representing himself.

When his mighty rival, Michelangelo, cast down that massive chisel which no one after him was worthy or able to wield, none survived him who could venture to repeat in marble the rugged grandeur of his countenance; but we imagine that we can trace in the head of some unfinished satyr, or in the sublime countenance of his Moses, the natural or the idealized type from which he drew his stern and noble inspirations.

And, to turn to another great art, when Mozart closed his last uncompleted score, and laid him down to pass from the regions of earthly to those of heavenly music, which none had so closely approached as he, the science over which he ruled could find no strains in which worthily to mourn him except his own, and was compelled to sing for the first time his own marvellous Requiem at his funeral.*

No less can it be said that when the pen dropped from Shakespeare's hand, when his last mortal illness mastered the strength of even his genius, the world was left powerless to describe in writing his noble and unrivalled characteristics. Hence we turn back upon himself, and endeavour to draw

---

* The same may be said of the celebrated Cimarosa.

from his own works the only true records of his genius and his mind.*

We apply to him phrases which he has uttered of others ; we believe that he must have involuntarily described himself, when he says,

> " Take him all in all,
> We shall not look upon his like again ;"

or that he must even consciously have given a reflection of himself when he so richly represents to us " the poet's eye in a fine phrenzy rolling." (" Midsummer Night's Dream," act v., scene 1.)

But in fact, considering that the character of a man is like that which he describes " as compounded of many simples extracted from many objects" (" As You Like It," act iv., scene 1), we naturally seek for those qualities which enter into his composition ; we look for them in his own

---

* Even in his lifetime this seems to have been foreseen. In 1664 an Epigram addressed to " Master William Shakespeare," and first published by Mr. Halliwell, occurred the following lines :—

" Besides in places thy wit windes like Mæander,
When (*whence*) needy new composers borrow more
Thence (*than*) Terence doth from Plautus or Menander,
But to praise thee aright I want thy store.
Then let thine owne words thine owne worth upraise
And help t' adorne thee with deserved baies."

Halliwell's Life of Shakespeare, p. 160.

pages ; we endeavour to cull from every part of his
works such attributions of great and noble qualities
to his characters, and unite them so as to form what
we believe is his truest portrait. In truth, no
other author has perhaps existed who has so completely reflected himself in his works as Shakespeare. For, as artists will tell us that every
great master has more or less reproduced in his
works characteristics to be found in himself, this is
far more true of our greatest dramatist, whose
genius, whose mind, whose heart, and whose entire
soul live and breathe in every page and every line
of his imperishable works. Indeed, as in these
there is infinitely greater variety, and consequently
greater versatility of power necessary to produce
it, so must the amount of elements which enter into
his composition represent changeable yet blending
qualities beyond what the most finished master
in any other art can be supposed to have possessed.

The positive and directly applicable materials
which we possess for constructing a biography of
this our greatest writer, are more scanty than
have been collected to illustrate the life of many
an inferior author. His contemporaries, his friends,
perhaps admirers, have left us but few anecdotes

of his life, and have recorded but few traits of either his appearance or his character. Those who immediately succeeded him seem to have taken but little pains to collect early traditions concerning him, while yet they must have been fresh in the recollections of his fellow-countrymen, and still more of his fellow-townsmen.*

It appears as though they were scarcely conscious of the great and brilliant luminary of English literature which was shining still, or had but lately passed away; and as though they could not anticipate either the admiration which was to succeed their

* As evidence of this neglect we may cite the "Journal" of the Rev. John Ward, Incumbent of Stratford-upon-Avon, to which he was appointed in 1662. This diary, which has been published by Doctor Severn, "from the original MSS.," preserved in the library of the Medical Society of London, contains but two pages relating to Shakespeare, and those contain but scanty and unsatisfactory notices. I will quote only two sentences:

"Remember to peruse Shakespeare's Plays—bee much versed in them, that I may not bee ignorant in that matter, whether Dr. Heylin does well, in reckoning up the dramatick poets which have been famous in England, to omit Shakespeare" (p. 184). Shakespeare's daughter was still alive when this was written, as appears from the sentence that immediately follows: it seems to us wonderful that so soon after the Poet's death a shrewd and clever clergyman and physician (for Mr. Ward was both) should have known so little about his celebrated townsman's works or life.

duller perceptions of his unapproachable grandeur, or the eager desire which this would generate, of knowing even the smallest details of its rise, its appearance, its departure. For by the biography of Shakespeare one cannot understand the records of what he bought, of what he sold, or the recital of those acts which only confound him with the common mass which surrounded him, and make him appear as the worthy burgess or the thrifty merchant; though even about the ordinary common-place portions of his life such uncertainty exists, that doubts have been thrown on the very genuineness of that house which he is supposed to have inhabited.

Now, it is the characteristic individualizing quality, actions, and mode of executing his works, to whatever class of excellence he may belong, that we long to be familiar with in order to say that we know the man. What matters it to us that he paid so many marks or shillings to purchase a homestead in Stratford-upon-Avon? The simple autograph of his name is now worth all the sums that he thus expended. One single line of one of his dramas, written in his own hand, would be worth to his admirers all the sums which are known to have passed between him and others.

What has become of the goodly folios which must
have once existed written in his own hand?
Where are the books annotated or even scratched
by his pen, from which he drew the subjects and
sometimes the substance of his dramas? What
Vandalism destroyed the first, or dispersed the
second of these valuable treasures? How is it
that we know nothing of his method of composition? Was it in solitude and sacred seclusion,
self-imprisoned for hours beyond the reach of the tur-
moil of the street or the domestic sounds of home?
Or were his unrivalled works produced in scraps
of time and fugitive moments, even perhaps in the
waiting-room of the theatre, or the brawling or
jovial sounds of the tavern?

Was he silent, thoughtful, while his fertile brain
was seething and heaving in the fermentation of
his glorious conceptions; so that men should have
said—" Hush! Shakespeare is at work with some
new and mighty imaginings!" or wore he always that
light and careless spirit which often belongs to the
spontaneous facility of genius; so that his comrades
may have wondered when, and where, and how his
grave characters, his solemn scenes, his fearful
catastrophes, and his sublime maxims of original
wisdom, were conceived, planned, matured, and

finally written down, to rule for ever the world of
letters? Almost the only fact connected with his
literary life which has come down to us is one
which has been recorded, perhaps with jealousy,
certainly with ill-temper, by his friend Ben Jonson—
that he wrote with overhaste, and hardly ever
erased a line, though it would have been better
had he done so with many.

This almost total absence of all external information, this drying-up of the ordinary channels of
personal history, forces us to seek for the character
and the very life of Shakespeare in his own works.
But how difficult, in analysing the complex consti-
tution of such a man's principles, motives, passions,
and affections, to discriminate between what he has
drawn from himself, and what he has created by
the force of his imagination. Dealing habitually
with fictions, sometimes in their noblest, sometimes
in their vilest forms—here gross and even savage,
there refined and sometimes ethereal, how shall we
discover what portions of them were copied from
the glass which he held before himself, what from
the magic mirrors across which flitted illusive or
fanciful imagery? The work seems hopeless. It
is not like that of the printer, who, from a chaotic
heap of seemingly unmeaning lead, draws out

letter after letter, and so disposes them that they shall make senseful and even brilliant lines. It is more like the hopeless labour of one who, from the fragments of a tessclated pavement, should try to draw the elegant and exquisitely tinted figure which once it bore.

This difficulty of appreciating, and still more of delineating, the character of our great poet, makes him, without perhaps an exception, the most difficult literary theme in English letters.

How to reduce the subject to a lecture seems indeed a literal paradox. But when to this difficulty is added that of an impossible compression into narrow limits of the widest and vastest compass ever embraced by any one man's genius, it must appear an excess of rashness in anyone to presume that he can do justice to the subject on which I am addressing you.

It seems, therefore, hardly wonderful that even the last year, dedicated naturally to the tercentenary commemoration of William Shakespeare, should have passed over without any public eulogy of his greatness, in this our metropolis. It seemed, indeed, as if the magnitude of that one man's genius was too oppressive for this generation. It was not, I believe, an undervaluing of his merits which produced the frustration of efforts, and the disappointment of expectations, that seemed to put to rout and confusion, or rather to paralyse the exertions so strenuously commenced to mark the year as a great epoch in England's literary history. I believe, on the contrary, that the dimensions of Shakespeare had grown so immeasurably in the estimation of his fellow-countrymen, that the proportions of his genius to all that had followed him, and all that surround us, had grown so enormously in the judgment and feeling of the country, from the nobleman to the workman, that the genius of the man oppressed us, and made us feel that all our multiplied resources of art and speech were unequal to his worthy commemoration. No plan proposed for this purpose seemed adequate to attain it. Nothing solid and permanent that could either come up to his merits or to our aspirations seemed to be within the grasp either of the arts or of the wealth of our country. The year has passed away, and Shakespeare remains without any monument, except that which, by his wonderful writings, he has raised for himself. Even the research after a site fit for the erection of a monument to him, in the city of squares, of gardens, and of parks, seemed only to work perplexity and hopelessness.

Presumptuous as it may appear, the claim to connect myself with that expired and extinct movement is my only apology for my appearing before you. If, a year after its time, I take upon myself the eulogy of Shakespeare, if I appear to come forward as with a funeral oration, to give him, in a manner, posthumous glory, it is because my work has dropped out of its place, and not because I have inopportunely misplaced it. In the course of the last year, it was proposed to me, both directly and indirectly, to deliver a lecture on Shakespeare. I was bold enough to yield my assent, and thus felt that I had contracted an obligation to the memory of the bard, as well as to those who thought that my sharing what was done for his honour would possess any value. A task undertaken becomes a duty unfulfilled. When, therefore, it was proposed to me to perform my portion of the homage which I considered due to him, though it was to be a month too late, I felt it would be cowardice to shrink from its performance.

For in truth the undertaking required some courage ; and to retire before its difficulties might be stigmatised as a dastardly timidity. It is a work of courage at any time and in any place to undertake a lecture upon Shakespeare, more in fact than to venture on the delivery of a series. The latter gives scope for the thousand things which one would wish to say—it affords ample space for apposite illustration, and it enables one to enrich the subject with the innumerable and inimitable beauties that are flung like gems or flowers over every page of his magnificent works. But in the midst of public, or rather universal, celebration of a national and secular festival in his honour, in the presence probably of the most finished literary characters in this highly-educated country, still more certainly before numbers of those whom the nation acknowledges as deeply read in the works of our poet as the most accomplished critic of any age has been in the writings of the Classics —men who have introduced into our literature a class-name—that of " Shakespearian scholars,"—to have ventured to speak on this great theme might seem to have required, not courage, but temerity. Why, it might have been justly asked, do none of those who have consumed their lives in the study of him, not page by page, but line by line, who have pressed his sweet fruits between their lips till they have absorbed all their lusciousness, who have made his words their study, his thoughts their

meditation, why does not one at least among them
stand forward now, and leave for posterity the
record of his matured observation? Perhaps I
may assign the reason which I have before, that
they know, too, the unapproachable grandeur of the
theme, and the rare powers which are required to
grasp and to hold it.

Be it so; but at any rate if in the presence of
others so much more capable it would have been
rash to speak, to express one's thoughts, when
there is no competition, may be pardonable at
least.

And yet, when everybody else is silent, it may be
very naturally asked have I a single claim to put
forward upon your attention and indulgence? I
think I may have *one*; though I fear that when I
mention it, it may be considered either a paradox
or a refutation of my pretensions. My claim, then,
to be heard and borne with is this—that I have
never in my life seen Shakespeare acted; I have
never heard his eloquent speeches declaimed by
gifted performers; I have not listened to his noble
poetry as uttered by the kings or queens of
tragedy; I have not witnessed his grand, richly-
concerted scenes endowed with life by the graceful
gestures, the classical attitudes, the contrasting

emotions, and the pointed emphasis of those who in modern times may be considered to have even added to that which his genius produced ; I know nothing of the original and striking readings or renderings of particular passages by masters of mimic art; I know him only on his flat page, as he is represented in immoveable, featureless, unemotional type.

Nor am I acquainted with him surrounded, perhaps sometimes sustained, but, at any rate, worthily adorned and enhanced in accessory beauty by the magic illusion of scenic decorations, the splendid pageantry which he simply hints at, but which, I believe, has been now realised to its most ideal exactness and richness—banquets, tournaments, and battles, with the almost deceptive accuracy of costume and of architecture. When I hear of all these additional ornaments hung around his noble works, the impression which they make upon my mind creates a deeper sense of amazement and admiration, how dramas written for the " Globe " Theatre, wretchedly lighted, incapable of grandeur, even from want of space, and without those mechanical and artistical resources which belong to a later age, should be capable of bearing all this additional weight of lustre and magnificence without its being necessary to alter a word, still less a passage, from their original delivery.* This exhibits the nicely-balanced point of excellence which is equally poised between simplicity and gorgeousness ; which can retain its power and beauty, whether stript to its barest form or loaded with exuberant appurtenances.

After having said thus much of my own probably unenvied position, I think I shall not be wrong in assuming that none of Shakespeare's enthusiastic admirers, one of whom I profess myself to be, and that few of my audience are in this

* The chorus, which serves as a prologue to " King Henry V.," shows how Shakespeare's own mind keenly felt the deficiencies of his time, and almost anticipatingly wrote for the effects which a future age might supply :

> " But pardon, gentles all,
> This flat unraised spirit that hath dar'd,
> On this unworthy scaffold, to bring forth
> So great an object. Can this cock-pit hold
> The vasty fields of France ? Or may we cram
> Within this wooden O the very casques
> That did affright the air at Agincourt.
>
> .   .   .   .
>
> Piece out our imperfections with your thoughts ;
> Into a thousand parts divide one man,
> And make imaginary puissance :
> Think, when we talk of horses, that ye see them
> Printing their proud hoofs i' the receiving earth ;
> For 'tis your thoughts that now must deck our kings."

exceptional position. They will probably consider this a disadvantage on my side ; and to some extent I must acknowledge it—for Shakespeare wrote to be acted, and not to be read.

But on the other hand is it not something to have approached this wonderful man, and to have communed with him in silence and in solitude, face to face, alone with him alone ; to have read and studied and meditated on him in early youth, without gloss or commentary, or preface or glossary ? For such was my good or evil fortune ; not during the still hours of night, but during that stiller portion of an Italian afternoon, when silence is deeper than in the night, under a bright and sultry sun, when all are at rest, all around you hushed to the very footsteps in a well-peopled house, except the unquelled murmuring of a fountain beneath orange trees, which mingled thus the most delicate of fragrance with the most soothing of sounds, both stealing together through the half-closed windows of wide and lofty corridors. Is there not more of that reverence and that relish which constitute the classical taste to be derived from the concentration of thought and feelings which the perusal of the simple unmarred and unoverlaid text procures ; when you can ponder on a verse, can linger over a word, can repeat mentally and even orally with your own deliberation and your own emphasis, whenever dignity, beauty, or wisdom invite you to pause, or compel you to ruminate?

In fact, were you desired to give your judgment on the refreshing water of a pure fountain, you would not care to taste it from a richly-jewelled and delicately-chased cup; you would not consent to have it mingled with the choicest wine, nor flavoured by a single drop of the most exquisite essence; you would not have it chilled with ice, or gently attempered by warmth. No, you would choose the most transparent crystal vessel, however homely; you would fill at the very cleft of the rock from which it bubbles fresh and bright, and drink it yet sparkling, and beading with its own air-pearls the walls of the goblet. Nay, is not an opposite course that which the poet himself censures as " wasteful, ridiculous excess?"

" To gild refined gold, to paint the lily;
To throw a perfume on the violet.

. . . .

Or with a taper light
To seek the beauteous eye of heaven to varnish."
("King John," act iv., scene 2.)

You will easily understand, from this long and almost apologetic preamble, in the first place, that

C

I take it for granted that I am addressing an audience which is not assembled to receive elementary or new information concerning England's greatest poet. On the contrary, I believe myself to stand before many who are able to judge, rather than merely accept, my opinions, and in the presence of an assembly exclusively composed of his admirers, thoroughly conversant with his works. A further consequence is this, that my lecture will not consist of extracts—still less of recitations of any of those beautiful passages which occur in every play of Shakespeare. The most celebrated of these are present to the mind of every English scholar, from his school-boy days to his maturer studies.

II.

It would be superfluous for a lecturer on Shakespeare to put to himself the question, What place do you intend to give to the subject of your discourse in the literature of England or of Europe? Whatever difference of opinion may exist elsewhere, I believe that in this country only one answer will be given. Among our native writers no one questions that Shakespeare is supremely pre-emi-nent, and most of us will probably assign him as lofty a position in the whole range of modern European literature. Perhaps no other nation possesses among its writers any one name to which there is no rival claims, nor even an approximation of equality, to make a balance against it. Were we to imagine in England a Walhalla erected to contain the effigies of great men, and were one especial hall to contain those of our most eminent dramatists, it must needs be so constructed as to have one central niche. Were a similar structure prepared in France, it would be natural to place in equal prominence at least two figures, or, in classical language, two different muses of Tragedy and of Comedy would have to be separately repre-sented. But in England, assign what place we may to those who have excelled in either branch in mimic art, the highest excellence in both would be found centered in one man ; and from him on either side would have to range the successful cultivators of the drama.

But this claim to so undisputed an elevation does not rest upon his merits only in this field of our literature. Shakespeare has established his claim to the noblest position in English literature on a wider and more solid basis than the mere composition of skilful plays could deserve. As the great master of our language, as almost its regenerator, quite its refiner—as the author whose use of a word stamps it with the mark of purest English coinage—whose employment of a phrase makes it household and proverbial—whose sententious sayings, flowing without effort from his mind, seem almost sacred, and are quoted as axioms or maxims indisputable—as the orator whose speeches, not only apt, but, natural to the lips from which they issue, are more eloquent than the discourses of senators or finished public speakers—as the poet whose notes are richer, more wondrously varied than those of the greatest professed bards—as the writer who has run through the most varied ways and to the greatest extent through every department of literature and learning, through the history of many nations, their domestic manners, their characteristics, and even their personal distinctives, and who seems to have visited every part of nature, to have intuitively studied the heavens and the earth—as the man, in fine, who has shown himself supreme in so many things, superiority in any one of which gains reputation in life and glory after death, he is pre-eminent above all, and beyond the reach of envy or jealousy.

And if no other nation can show us another man whose head rises above all their other men of letters, as Shakespeare does over ours, they cannot pretend, by the accumulation of separated excellences, to put in competition with him a type rather than a realization of possible worth. Until, therefore, some other writer can be produced, no matter from what nation, who unites in himself personally these gifts of our bard in an equally sublime degree, his stature overtops them all, wherever born and however celebrated.

The question, however, may be raised—Is he so securely placed upon his pedestal that a rival may not one day thrust him from it?—is he so secure upon his throne that a rebel may not usurp it? To these interrogations I answer unhesitatingly—Yes.

In the first place, there have only been two poets in the world before Shakespeare who have attained the same position with him. Each came at the moment which closed the volume of the period past and opened that of a new epoch. Of what preceded Homer we can know but little; the songs by bards or rhapsodists had, no doubt, preceded him, and prepared the way for the first and greatest epic. This, it is acknowledged, has never been

surpassed; it became the standard of language, the
steadfast rule of versification, and the model of
poetical composition. His supremacy, once attained,
was shaken by no competition; it was as well assured after a hundred years as it has been by thousands. Dante again stood between the remnants
of the old Roman civilization and the construction
of a new and Christian system of arts and letters.
He, too, consolidated the floating fragments of an
indefinite language, and with them built and
thence himself fitted and adorned that stately
vessel which bears him through all the regions of
life and of death, of glory, of trial, and of perdi-
tion.

A word found in Dante is classical to the Italian
ear; a form, however strange in grammar, traced
to him, is considered justifiable if used by any
modern sonneteer.*   He holds the place in his
own country which Shakespeare does in ours; not
only is his *terza rima*, considered inimitable, but the
concentration of brilliant imagery in our words,
the flashes of his great thoughts and the copious
variety of his learning, marvellous in his age, make
his volume be to this day the delight of every

* Any one acquainted with Mastrofini's "Dictionary of
Italian Verbs" will understand this.

refined intelligence and every polished mind in Italy.

And he, too, like Homer, notwithstanding the magnificent poets who succeeded him, has never for a moment lost that fascination which he alone exercises over the domain of Italian poetry. He was as much its ruler in his own age as he is in the present.

In like manner the two centuries and more which have elapsed since Shakespeare's death have as completely confirmed him in his legitimate command as the same period did his two only real predecessors. No one can possibly either be placed in a similar position or come up to his great qualities, except at the expense of the destruction of our present civilization, the annihilation of its past traditions, the resolution of our language into jargon, and its regeneration, by a new birth, into something "more rich and strange" than the powerful idiom which so splendidly combines the Saxon and the Norman elements. Should such a devastation and reconstruction take place, whether they come from New Zealand or from Siberia, then there may spring up the poet of that time and condition who may be the fourth in that great series of unrivalled bards, but will no more inter-

fere with his predecessor's rights than Dante or
Shakespeare does with those of Homer.

But further, we may truly say that the legislator
of a people can be but one, and, as such, can
have no rival beyond his own shores. Solon,
Lycurgus, and Numa are the only three men in
profane history who have reached the dignity of
this singular title. The first seized on the character of the bland and polished Athenians, and
framed his code in such harmony with it, that no
subsequent laws, even in the periods of most cor-
rupt relaxation, could efface their primitive
stamp, cease to make the Republic proud of their
lawgiver's name.

Lycurgus understood the stern and almost
savage hardihood and simplicity of the Spartan
disposition, and perpetuated it and regulated it by
his harsh and unfeeling system, of which, notwithstanding which, the Lacedæmonian was proud. And
so Numa Pompilius comprehended the readiness of
the infant Republic, sprung from so doubtful and
discreditable a parentage, to discover a noble descent, and connect its birth and education with gods
and heroes, took hold of this weakness for the
sanction of his legislation, and feigned his confer-
ences with the nymph Egeria as the sources of his

wisdom.   No ; whatever may become of kings,
legislators are never dethroned.

And so is Shakespeare the unquestioned legislator of modern literary art.   No one will contend
that, without certain detriment, it would be possible for a modern writer, especially of dramatic
fiction, to go back beyond him and endeavour to
establish a pre-Shakesperian School of English
literature, as we have the pre-Raphaelite in art.
Struggle and writhe as any genius may—even if
endowed with giant strength—it will be but as the
battle of the Titans against Jove.   Huge rocks will
be rolled down upon him, and the lightning from
Shakespeare's hand will assuredly tear his laurels,
if it do not strike his head.   Byron could not appre-
ciate the dramatic genius of Shakespeare ; perhaps
his sympathies ranged more freely among Corsairs
and Suliotes than among purer and nobler spirits.
Certainly he speaks of him with a superciliousness
which betrays his inability fully to comprehend
him.*   And yet would " Manfred " have existed if

---

* Lord Byron thus writes to Mr. Murray, July 14th,
1821 :—   " I trust that Sardanapalus will not be mistaken
for a political play. . . . . You will find all this very
unlike Shakespeare ; and so much the better, in one sense,
for I look upon him to be the worst of models, though the
most extraordinary of writers."—MOORE'S *Life of Lord Byron.*

the romantic drama and the spirit-agency of
Shakespeare had not given it life and rule? So in
other nations. I shall probably quote to you the
sentiments of foreign writers of highest eminence
concerning Shakespeare, not as authorities, but
as illustrations of what I may say.

Singularly enough, the greatest of German
modern writers has nowhere recorded a full and
deliberate opinion on our poet. But who can
doubt that "Götz von Berlichingen with the Iron
Hand," and even the grand and tender "Faust,"
and no less Schiller's " Wallenstein," belong to the
family of Shakespeare, are remotely offsprings of his
genius, and have to be placed as tributary garlands
round his pedestal. To imagine Shakespeare even
in intention removed from his sovereignty, would
be a treachery parallel only to that of *Lear* dethroned by his own daughters.

But still more may we say that, in all such posi-
tions as that which we have assigned to Shakespeare,
there has always been a culminating point to
which succeeds decline—if not downfall. It is so
in art. Immediately after the death of Raphael,
and the dispersion of his school, art took a down-
ward direction, and has never risen again to the
same height. And while he marks the highest

elevation ever reached in the arts of Europe, a
similar observation will apply to their particular
schools. Leonardo and Luini in Lombardy; the
Carracci in Bologna; Fra Angelico in Umbria;
Garofalo in Ferrara, not only take the place of
chiefs in their respective districts, but mark the
period from which degeneracy has to date. And
so surely is it in our case, whatever may have been
the course of literature which led up to Shakespeare, without pronouncing judgment on Spenser,
or "rare Ben Jonson," it is certain that after him,
although England has possessed great poets, there
stands not one forward among them as Shakespeare's competitor. Milton, and Dryden, and
Addison, and Rowe have given us specimens of
high dramatic writing of no mean quality; others
as well, and even these have written much and
nobly, in lofty as in familiar verse; yet not one has
the public judgment of the nation placed on a level
with him. The intermediate space from them to
our own times has left only the traces of a weak
and enervated school. It would be unbecoming to
speak disparagingly of the poets of the present age;
but no one, I believe, has ventured to consider
them as superior to the noble spirits of our Augus-

tan age. The easy descent from the loftiest eminence is not easily reclimbed.

Surely, then, we may consider Shakespeare, as
an ancient mythologist would have done, as " en-
skied " among " the invulnerable clouds," where
no shaft, even of envy, can assail him. From this
elevation we may safely predict that he never can
be plucked.

III.

The next point which seems to claim attention
is the very root of all that I have said, or shall
have still to say. To what does Shakespeare owe
this supremacy, or whence flow all the extraordinary qualities which we attribute to him? You
are all prepared with the answer in one single
word—his GENIUS.

The genius of Shakespeare is our familiar
thought and ready expression when we study him,
and when we characterise him. Nevertheless,
simple and intelligible as is the word, it is ex-
tremely difficult to analyse or to define it. Yet
everything that is great and beautiful in his
writings seems to require an explanation of the
cause to which it owes its origin.

One great characteristic of genius easily and universally admitted is, that it is a gift, and not an acquisition. It belongs inherently to the person possessing it ; it cannot be transmitted by heritage ; it cannot be infused by parental affection ; it cannot be bestowed by earliest care ; neither can it be communicated by the most finished culture or the most studied education. It must be congenital, or rather inborn to its possessor. It is as much a living, a natural power, as is reason to every man. As surely as the very first germ of the plant contains in itself the faculty of one day evolving from itself leaves, flowers, and fruit, so does genius hold, however hidden, however unseen, the power to open, to bring forth, and to mature what other men cannot do, but what to it is instinctive and almost spontaneous. It may begin to manifest itself with the very dawn of reason ; it may remain asleep for years, till a spark, perhaps accidentally, kindles up into a sudden and irrepressible splendour, that unseen intellectual fuel which has been almost unknown to its unambitious owner.

In our own minds we easily distinguish between the highest abilities or the most rare attainments, when the fruit of education and of application, and what we habitually distinguish as the manifestation of genius. But still we do not find it so easy to reduce to words this mental distinction; the one, after all, however gracefully and however brightly, walks upon the earth, adorning it by the good or fair things which it scatters on its way; the other has wings, and flies above the surface—it is like the aurora of Homer or of Thorwaldsen, which, as it flies above the plane of mortal actions, sheds down its flowers along its brilliant path, upon those worthy to gaze upwards towards it. We connect in our minds with genius the ideas of flashing splendour and eccentric movement. It is an intellectual meteor, the laws of which cannot be defined or reduced to any given theory. We regard it with a certain awe, and leave it to soar or to droop, to shine or disappear, to dash irregularly first in one direction and then in another; no one dare curb it or direct it; but all feel sure that its course, however inexplicable, is subject to higher and controlling rule. But in order to define more closely what we in reality understand by genius, it may be well to consider its action in divided and more restricted spheres of activity. For although we habitually attribute this singular quality to many, and often but on light grounds, it is seldom that we do so seriously and deliberately without some qualifying epithet. We speak of a military genius, of a mechanical genius, of a poetical genius, of a musical genius, or of an artistic genius. All these expressions contain a restrictive clause. We do not understand when we use them that the person to whom they were attributed possessed any power beyond the limits of a particuler sphere. We do not mean by the use of the word genius that the soldier knew anything of poetry, or the printer of mechanism. We understand that each in his own profession or stage of excellence possessed a complete elevation over the bulk of those who followed the same pursuits ; a superiority so visible, so acknowledged, and so clearly individual, that no one else considered it inferiority, still less felt shame at not being able to rise to the same level. They gather round them acknowledged disciples and admirers, who rather glory to have been guided by their teaching, and formed on their example.

And in what consisted that complete though limited excellence? If I might venture to express a judgment, I would say that genius in these different courses of science or art may be defined a natural sympathy with all that relates to each of them, with the power of giving full and certain execution to the mental conception. The military genius is one who, either untrained by studious preparation, or else starting out of the lines in which many were ranged level with himself, seizes the staff of command, and receives the homage of comrades and superiors. While others have been plodding through the long drill of theory and of practice, he is found to have discovered a new system of the science, bold, irregular, but successful. But to possess this genius, there must be a universal sympathy with all that relates to its own peculiar province. The military genius of which we are speaking must embrace or acquire that which relates to the soldier's life and duty, from the *dress* of the single soldier, from his duties in the sentry-box, or on the picquet, to the practice of the regiment and the evolutions of a field-day ; from the complete command of tens of thousands on the battle-field, with an eagle's eye and a lion's heart, to the scientific planning, on the chessboard of an empire, of the campaign, which he meditates move by move and check by check, till the final victory is crowned in the capital city. He who has not given proof of his being equal to all this, has not made good his claim to military

genius. But such a one will find, wherever he
puts his hand, generals and marshals, each able to
command a host, or to take his place in his rough-
est of enterprises.

I need not pass through other forms of genius to
reach similar results ; Stephenson, from the labour of
the mine, creating that system of mechanical motion,
which may be said to have subdued the world, and
bound the earth in iron links; Mozart, giving
concerts at the age of seven, that astonished grey-
headed musicians; Raphael, before the ordinary
age of finished pupilage, master of every known
detail in art of oil or fresco, drawing, expression, and
grand composition ; Giotto, caught in the field as a
young shepherd by Cimabue, drawing his sheep upon
a stone, and soon becoming the master of modern
art.* These and many others repeat to us what I
have said of the military genius—an inborn capa-
city, comprehensive and complete, with the power

---

* The early manifestation of artistic power is so frequent
and well known, that it would be superfluous to enumerate
other instances. The expression " *anch' io son pittore*" is
become proverbial. One of the Carracci, on being translated
from an inferior profession to the family studio, was found
at once to possess the pictorial skill of his race. At the present, Mintropp at Düsseldorf, and Ackermann at Berlin,
are both instances of very high artists, the one in drawing
the other in sculpture, both originally shepherds.

of fully carrying out the suggestions of mind. Had there been a single portion of their pursuits in which they did not excel, if the result of their work had not exhibited the happy union and concord of the many qualities requisite for its perfection, they never would have attained the attribution of genius.

If this sympathy with one branch of higher pursuits passes beyond it and associates with it a similar facility of acquisition and execution in some other and distinct art or science, it is clear that the claim to genius is higher and more extensive. Raphael was before the world a painter, but he could scarcely have been so without embracing every other department of art. Before the science of perspective was matured or popularly known, when, in consequence, defects are to be found in the disposition of figures, and in the adjustment of aerial distances,* his architecture shows an instinctive familiarity with its rules and proportions; a proof that he possessed an architectural eye. And consequently the one statue which he is supposed to have carved, and the one palace which he is

* See Mr. Lloyd's article on " Raphael's School of Athens," in Mr. Woodward's *Fine Art Quarterly Review*, January 1864, p. 67.

said to have built, show how easily he could have undertaken and executed beautiful works in either of those two classes of art.   In Orcagna and Michelangelo we have the three branches of art supremely united; and the second of these adds poetry and literature to his artistic excellence.   In like manner, Leonardo has left proof of most varied and accurate mechanical as well as literary genius.

It is evident, however, that while a genius has its point of concentration, every remove from this, though wider, will be fainter and less complete. We may describe it as Shakespeare himself describes glory, and say :

> " *Genius* is like a circle in the water,
>   Which never ceaseth to enlarge itself,
>   Till, by broad spreading, it disperse to naught."
>   ("Henry VI.," act i., scene 3.)

The sympathies with more remote subjects and pursuits will be rather the means of illustration, adornment, and pleasing variety, than for the essential requirements of the principal aim.   But though less minute in their application, in the hand of genius they will be wonderfully accurate and apt.

IV.

All that I have been saying is applicable in the most complete and marvellous way to Shakespeare's genius. His sympathies are universal, perfect in their own immediate use, infinitely varied, and strikingly beautiful, when they reach remoter objects. And hence, though at first sight he might be classified among those who have displayed a literary genius, he stretches his mind and his feelings so beyond them on every side, that to him, almost, perhaps, beyond any other man, the simple distinctive, without any qualification, belongs. No one need fear to call Shakespeare simply a grand, a sublime genius.

The centre-point of his sympathies is clearly his dramatic art. From this they expand, for many degrees, with scarce perceptible diminution, till they lose themselves in far distant, and, to him, un-explored space. This nucleus of his genius has certainly never been equalled before or since. Its essence consists in what is the very soul of the dramatic idea, the power to throw himself into the situation, the circumstances, the nature, the acquired habits, the feelings, true or fictitious, of every character which he introduces. This forms, in fact, the most perfect of sympathies. We do not, of course, use the word in that more usual sense of harmony of affection, or consent of feeling. Shakespeare has sympathy as complete for *Shylock* or *Iago*, as he has for *Arthur*, or *King Lear*. For a time he lives in the astute villain as in the inno- cent child ; he works his entire power of thought into intricacies of the traitor's brain ; he makes his heart beat in concord with the usurer's sanguinary spite, and then, like some beautiful creature in the animal world, draws himself out of the hateful evil, and is himself again ; and able, even, often to hold his own noble and gentle qualities as a mirror, or exhibit the loftiest, the most generous, and amiable examples of our nature. And this is all done with- out study, and apparently without effort. His infinitely varied characters come naturally into their places, never for a moment lose their pro- prieties, their personality, and the exact flexibility which results from the necessary combination in every man of many qualities. From the beginning to the end each one is the same, yet reflecting in himself the lights and shadows which flit around him.

This extraordinary versatility stands in striking

contrast with the dramatic productions of other countries. The Greek tragedian is Greek throughout—his subjects, his mythology, his sentences, play wonderfully indeed, but yet restrictedly, within a given sphere. And Rome is but the imitator in all its literature of its great mistress and model.

> " Graiis eloquium, Graiis dedit ore rotundo,
> Musa loqui."

Even through the French school, with the strict adhesion to the ancient rule of the unities, seems to have descended the partiality for what may be called the chastely classical subjects. Not so with Shakespeare.

Who, a stranger might ask, is the man, and where was he born, and where did he live, that not only his acts and scenes are placed in any age, or in any land, but that he can fill his stage with the very living men of the time and place represented, make them move as easily as if he held them in strings ; and make them speak not only with general conformity to their common position, but with individual and distinctive propriety, so that each is different from the rest ?   Did he live in ancient Rome, strolling the Forum, or climbing the Capitol ; hear ancient matrons converse with modest dignity ;

listen to conspirators among the columns of its porticos ; mingle among senators round Pompey's statue ; or with plebeians crowding to hear Brutus or Antony harangue ? Was he one accustomed to idle in the Piazza of St. Mark, or shoot his gondola under the Rialto ? Or was he a knight or even archer in the fields of France or England during the period of the Plantagenets or Tudors, and witnessed and wrote down the great deeds of those times, and knew intimately and personally each puissant lord who distinguished himself by his valour, by his wisdom, or even by his crimes ? Did he live in the courts of princes, perchance holding some office which enabled him to listen to the grave utterances of kings and their counsellors, or to the witty sayings of court jesters ? Did he consort with banished princes, and partake of their sports or their sufferings ? In fine, did he live in great cities, or in shepherds' cottages, or in fields and woods ; and does he date from John and live on to the eighth Henry—a thread connecting in himself the different epochs of mediæval England ? One would almost say so ; or multiply one man into many, whose works have been united under one man.

This ubiquity, if we may so call it, of Shake-

speare's sympathies, constitutes the unlimited
extent and might of his dramatic genius. It would
be difficult to imagine where a boundary line could
at length have been drawn, beyond which nothing
original, nothing new, and nothing beautiful, could
be supposed to have come forth from his mind.
We are compelled to say that his genius was inexhaustible.

V.

This rare and wonderful faculty becomes more
interesting if we follow it into further details.

I remember an anecdote of Garrick, who, in
company with another performer of some eminence,
was walking in the country, and about to enter a
village. "Let us pass off," said the younger
comedian to his more distinguished companion,
"as two intoxicated fellows." They did so,
apparently with perfect success, being saluted
by the jeers and abuse of the inhabitants. When
they came forth at the other end of the village, the
younger performer asked Garrick how he had ful-
filled his part. "Very well," was the reply,
"except that you were not perfectly tipsy in your
legs."

Now, in Shakespeare there is no danger of a
similar defect. Whatever his character is intended
to be, it is carried out to its very extremities.
Nothing is forgotten, nothing overlooked. Many
of you, no doubt, are aware that a controversy has
long existed, whether the madness of *Hamlet* is
intended by Shakespeare to be real or simulated.
If a dramatist wished to represent one of his persons as feigning madness, that assumed condition
would be naturally desired by the writer to be as
like as possible to the real affliction. If the other
persons associated with him could at once discover
that the madness was put on, of course the entire
action would be marred, and the object for which
the pretended madness was designed would be de-
feated by the discovery. How consummate must
be the poet's art, who can have so skilfully described, to the minutest symptoms, the mental
malady of a great mind, as to leave it uncertain to
the present day, even among learned physicians
versed in such maladies, whether *Hamlet's* madness
was real or assumed.

This controversy may be said to have been brought
to a close by one of the ablest among those in England who have every opportunity of studying the
almost innumerable shades through which aliena-

tion of mind can pass.* And so delicate are the
changeful characteristics which Shakespeare describes, that Dr. Conolly considers that a twofold
form of disease is placed before us in the Danish
prince. He concludes that he was labouring under
real madness, yet able to put on a fictitious and
artificial derangement for the purposes which he
kept in view. Passing through act by act and
scene by scene, analysing, with experienced eye,
each new symptom as it occurs, dividing and
anatomatising, with the finest scalpel, every fibre
of his brain. He exhibits, step by step, the tran-
sitionary characters of the natural disease in a
mind naturally, and by education, great and noble,
but thrown off his pivot by the anguish of his
sufferings and the strain of aroused passion. And
to this is superadded another and not genuine
affection, which serves its turn with that estranged
mind when it suits it to act, more especially that
part which the natural ailment did not suffice for.

---

* "A Study of Hamlet," by John Conolly, M.D., London,
1863. In p. 52 the author quotes Mr. Coleridge and M.
Killemain as holding the opinion that Shakespeare has "con-
trived to blend both (feigned and real madness) in the extraordinary character of *Hamlet*; and to join together the
light of reason, the cunning of intentional error, and the in-
voluntary disorder of a soul."

Now, Dr. Conolly considers these symptoms so accurately as well as minutely described, that he
throws out the conjecture that Shakespeare may
have borrowed the account of them from some unknown papers by his son-in-law, Dr. Hall.

But let it be remembered that in those days
mental phenomena were by no means accurately
examined or generally known. There was but
little attention paid to the peculiar forms of mono-
mania, or to its treatment, beyond restraint and
often cruelty. The poor idiot was allowed, if
harmless, to wander about the village or the
country to drivel or gibber amidst the teasing or
ill-natured treatment of boys or rustics. The poor
maniac was chained or tied in some wretched out-
house, at the mercy of some heartless guardian,
with no protector but the constable. Shakespeare
could not be supposed, in the little town of Stratford, nor indeed in London itself, to have had opportunities of studying the influence and the appearance of mental derangement of a high-minded and
finely-cultivated prince. How then did Shakespeare contrive to paint so highly-finished and yet
so complex an image? Simply by the exercise of
that strong sympathetic will which enabled him to
transport, or rather to transmute, himself into

another personality. While this character was
strongly before him he changed himself into a
maniac; he felt intuitively what would be his own
thought, what his feelings, were he in that situation;
he played with himself the part of the madman,
with his own grand mind as the basis of its action;
he grasped on every side the imagery which he felt
would have come into his mind, beautiful even
when dislorded, sublime even when it was grovel-
ling, brilliant even when dulled, and clothed it in
words of fire and of tenderness, with a varied
rapidity which partakes of wildness and of sense.
He needed not to look for a model out of himself,
for it cost him no effort to change the angle of his
mirror and sketch his own countenance awry. It
was but little for him to pluck away the crown
from reason and contemplate it dethroned.

Before taking leave of Dr. Conolly's most interesting
monography, I will allow myself to make only one
remark. Having determined to represent *Hamlet*
in this anomalous and perplexing condition, it was
of the utmost importance to the course and end of
this sublime drama, that one principal incident should
be most decisively separated from *Hamlet's* reverse
of mind. Had it been possible to attribute
the appearance of the *Ghost*, as the *Queen*,

his mother, does attribute it in the fifth act,
to the delusion of his bewildered phantasy, the
whole groundwork of the drama would have
crumbled beneath its superincumbent weight.
Had the spectre been seen by *Hamlet*, or by him
first, we should have been perpetually troubled
with the doubt whether or not it was the hallucina-
tion of a distracted, or the invention of a deceitful
brain. But Shakespeare felt the necessity of making
this apparition be held for a reality, and therefore
he makes it the very first incident in his tragedy,
antecedent to the slightest symptom of either
natural or affected derangement, and makes it first
be seen by two witnesses together, and then con-
jointly by a third unbelieving and fearless witness.
It is the testimony of these three which first
brings to the knowledge of the incredulous prince
this extraordinary occurrence. One may doubt
whether any other writer has ever made a ghost
appear successively to those whom we may call the
wrong persons, before showing himself to the one
whom alone he cared to visit. The extraordinary
exigencies of Shakespeare's plot rendered necessary
this unusual fiction. And it serves, moreover,
to give the only colour of justice to acts which

otherwise must have appeared unqualified as mad freaks or frightful crimes.

What Dr. Conolly has done for *Hamlet* and *Ophelia*, Dr. Bucknill had previously performed on a more extensive scale. In his " Psychology of Shakespeare,"* he has minutely investigated the mental condition of *Macbeth, King Lear, Timon,* and other characters. On *Hamlet* he seems inclined to take a different view from Dr. Conolly ; inasmuch as he considers the simulated madness the principal feature, and the natural unsoundness which it is impossible to overlook as secondary. But this eminent physician, well known for his extensive studies of insanity, bears similar testimony to the extraordinary accuracy of Shakespeare's delineations of mental diseases ; the nicety with which he traces their various steps in one individual, the accuracy with which he distinguishes these morbid affections in different persons. He seems unable to account for the exact minuteness in any other way than by external observation. He acknowledges that "indefinable possession of genius, call it spiritual tact or insight, or whatever term may suggest itself, by which the great lords of mind estimate all phases of mind with little

* Page 58 and 100.

aid from reflected light," as the mental instrument
through which Shakespeare looked upon others
at a distance, or within reach of minute observation.
Still he seems to think that Shakespeare must have
had many opportunities of observing mental phenomena. I own I am more inclined to think that the
process by which the genius of Shakespeare reached
this painful yet strange accuracy was rather that
of introversion than of external observation. At
any rate, it is most interesting to see eminent physicians maintaining by some means or other that
Shakespeare arrived by some sort of intuition at
the possession of a psychological or even medical
knowledge, fully verified and proved to be exact
by the researches two centuries later of distinguished
men in a science only recently developed. Mrs. -
Jameson has well distinguished the different forms
of mental aberration in Shakespeare's characters,
when she says that " *Constance* is frantic, *Lear* is
mad, *Ophelia* is insane."*

VI.

This last quotation may serve to introduce a

* *Characteristics of Women.* New York, 1833, p. 142.

further and a more delicate test of Shakespeare's insight into character. That a man should be able to throw himself into a variety of mind and characters among his fellow-men, may be not unreasonably expected. He has naturally a community of feelings, of passions, of temptations, and of motives with them. He can understand what is courage, what ambition, what strength or feebleness of mind. Inward observation and matured experience help much to guide him to a conception and a delineation of the character of his fellow-men. But of the stronger emotions, the wilder passions, the subdued gentleness and tenderness, the heroic endurance, the meek bearing, and the saintly patience of the woman, he can have had no experience. Looking into himself for a reflection, he will probably find a blank.

It has often been said that in his female characters Shakespeare is not equal to himself. The work to which I have just alluded meets, I think, completely, this objection, which, I believe, even Schlegel raises. It required a lady, with mind highly cultivated, with the nicest powers of discrimination, and with happiness of expression, to vindicate at once Shakespeare and her sex. The difficulty of this task can hardly be appreciated

without the study of its performance. Its great
difficulty consists in the almost family resemblance
of the different portraits which make up Shakespeare's female gallery. There is scarcely any
room for events, even for incident, still less for
actions, say for bold and unfeminine deeds.
Several of the heroines of Shakespeare are sub-
jected to similar persecutions, and almost the same
trials. In almost every one the affections
and their expression have alone to interest us.
From *Miranda*, the desert-nurtured child in the
simplicity of untempted innocence, to *Isabella*, in
her cloistered virtue, or *Hermione*, in her unyield-
ing fortitude—there are such shades, such vary-
ing yet delicate tints, that not two of these numerous conceptions can be said to resemble another.
And whence did Shakespeare derive his models?
Some are lofty queens, others most noble ladies,
some foreigners, some native; different types in
mind and heart, as in the lineament or complexion.
Where did he find them? Where did he meet
them? In the cottages of Stratford, or in the
purlieus of Blackfriars? Among the ladies of the
Court, or in the audience in his pit? No one can
say—no one need say. They were the formations
of his own quickened and fertile brain, which required

E

but one stroke, one line, to sketch him a portrait to
which he would give immortality. Far more difficult was this success, and not less completely was it
achieved, in that character which medical writers
seem hardly to believe could be but a conception.
We may compare the mind of Shakespeare to a
diamond pellucid, bright, and untinted, cut into
countless polished facets, which, in constant movement, at every smallest change of direction or of
angle, caught a new reflection, so that not one
of its brilliant mirrors could be for a moment idle,
but by a power beyond its control was ever busy
with the reflection of innumerable images, either
distinct or running into one another, or repeated
each so clearly as to allow him, when he chose, to
fix it in his memory.

VII.

We may safely conclude that, in whatever constitutes the dramatic art in its strictest sense,
Shakespeare possessed matchless sympathies with
all its attributes. The next and most essential
quality required for true genius is the power to
give outward life to the inward conception. With-

out this the poet is dumb. He may be a "mute inglorious Milton"; he cannot be a speaking, noble Shakespeare. I should think that I was almost insulting such an audience, were I to descant upon Shakespeare's position among the bards and writers of England, and of the modern world. Upon this point there can scarcely be a dissentient opinion. His language is the purest and best, his verses the most flowing and rich; and as for his sentiments, it would be difficult without the command of his own language to characterise them. No other writer has ever given such periods of sententious wisdom.

. . . .

I have spoken of genius as a gift to an individual man. I will conclude by the reflection that that man becomes himself a gift; a gift to his nation; a gift to his age; a gift to the world of all times. That same Providence which bestows greatness, majesty, abundance, and grace, no less presents, from time to time, to a people or a race, these few transcendent men who mark for it periods no less decisively, though more nobly, than victories or conquests. On England that supreme power has lavished the choicest blessings of this worldly life;

it has made it vast in dominion, matchless in strength; it has made it the arbiter of the earth, and mistress of the sea; it has made it able to stretch its arm for war to the savage antipodes, and, if it chose, its hand for peace to the utter civilised West; it has brought the produce of North and South to its feet with skill and power, to transform and to refashion in forms graceful or useful, to send them back, almost as new creations, to its very source. Industry has clothed its most barren plains with luxuriant crops; and with Titan boldness hollowed its sternest rocks, to plunder them of their ever-hidden treasures. Its gigantic strength seems but to play with every work of venturesome enterprise, till its cities seem to the stranger to overflow with riches, and its country to be overspread with exuberant prosperity.

Well, these are great and magnificent favours of an overruling, most benignant Power; and yet there is a boast which belongs to our country that may seem to be overlooked. Yet it is a double gift that that same creating and directing rule has made this country the birthplace and the seat of the two men who, within a short period, were made the rulers each of a great and separate intellectual dominion, never to be deposed, never to be rivalled,

never to be envied. To Newton was given the
sway over the science of the civilised world ; to
Shakespeare the sovereignty over its literature.

The one stands before us passionless and grave,
embracing in his intellectual grandeur every portion of
the universe, from the stars, to him invisible, to the
rippling of the tiny waves which the tide brought
to his feet. The host of heaven, that seemed in
causeless dispersion, he marshalled into order, and
bound in safest discipline. He made known to his
fellow-men the secret laws of heaven, the springs of
movement, and the chains of connection, which
invariably and unchangeably impel and guide the
course of its many worlds.

In this aspect one's imagination figures him as
truly the director of what he only describes—as the
leader of a complicated army, who, with his staff,
seems to draw or to send forward the wheeling bat-
talions, intent on their own errands, combining or
resolving movements far remote ; or, under a more
benign and pleasing form, we may contemplate him,
like a great master in musical science, standing in
the midst of a throng, in which are mingled together the elements of sublimest harmonies, confused to the eye, but sweetly attuned to the ear,
mingling into orderly combination and flowing

sequence, as they float through the air, which, though he elicit not nor produce, he seems by his outstretched hand to direct, or, at least, he proves himself fully to understand. For what each one separately does, unconscious of what even his companion is doing, he from afar knows, and almost beholds, understanding from his centre the concerted and sure results of their united action. And so Newton, from his chamber on this little earth, without being able more than the most helpless insect to add power or give guidance to one single element in the composition of this universe, could trace the orbits of planet or satellite, and calculate the oscillations and the reciprocal influences of celestial spheres.

Then his directing wand seems to contract itself to a space within his grasp. It becomes that magic prism with which he intercepts a ray from the sun on his passage to earth ; and as a bird seizes in its flight the bee laden with its honey, and robs it of its sweet treasure—even so he compels the messenger of light to unfold itself before us, and lay bare to our sight the rich colours which the rainbow had exhibited to man since the deluge, and which had lain concealed since creation, in every sunbeam that had passed through our atmosphere. And

further still, he bequeathes that wonderful alembic
of light to succeeding generations, till, in the hand
of new discoverers, it has become the key of Nature's laboratory, in which she has been surprised
melting and compounding, in crucibles huge as
ocean, the rich hues with which she overlays the
surfaces of suns and stars, yet, at the same time,
breathes its delicate blush upon the tenderest petals
of the opening rose.

And all the laws and all the rules which form
his code of nature seem engraved, as with a diamond point, upon a granite surface of the primitive rocks—inflexible, immoveable, unchangeable as
the system which they represent.

Beside him stands the Ruler of that world,
which, though even sublimely intellectual, is go-
verned by him with laws in which the affections,
even the passions, the moralities, and the anxieties
of life have their share; in which there is no seve-
rity but for vice, no slavery but for baseness, no
unforgivingness but for calculating wickedness.
In his hand is not the staff of authority; whether
it take the form of a royal sceptre or of a knightly
lance, whether it be the shepherdess's crook or the
fool's bauble, it is still the same, the magician's
wand. Whether it be the divining rod with which

he draws up to light the most hidden streams of nature's emotions, or the potential instrument of *Prospero's* spells, which raises storms in the deep or works spirit-music in the air, or the wicked implement with which the witches mingle their unholy charm, its cunning and its might have no limit among created things. But it is not a world of stately order which he rules, nor are the laws of unvarying rigour by which it is commanded. The wildest paroxysms of passion, the softest delicacy of emotions; the most extravagant accident of fortune, the tenderest incidents of home; the king and the beggar, the sage and the jester, the tyrant and his victim; the maiden from the cloister and the peasant from the mountains; the Italian school-child and the Roman matron; the princes of Denmark and the lords of Troy—all these and much more are comprised in the vast embrace of his dominions. Scarcely a rule can be drawn from them, yet each forms a model separately, a finished group in combination. Unconsciously as he weaves his work, apparently without pattern or design, he interlaces and combines in its surface and its depth images of the most charming variety and beauty; now the stern mosaic, without colouring, of an ancient pavement, now the flowing and intertwining arabesque of the fanciful east; now the rude scenes of ancient mediæval tapestry like that of Beauvais, and then the finished and richly tinted production of the Gobelins loom.

And yet through this seeming chaos the light permeates, and that so clear and so brilliant as equally to define and to dazzle. Every portion, every fragment, every particle, stands forth separate and particular, so as to be handled, measured, and weighed in the balance of critic and poet. Each has its own exact form and accurate place, so that, while separately they are beautiful, united they are perfect. Hence their combinations have become sacred rules, and have given inviolable maxims not only to English but to universal literature. Germany, as we have seen, studies with love and almost veneration every page of Shakespeare; national sympathies and kindred speech make it not merely easy but natural to all people of the Teutonic family to assimilate their literature to that its highest standard. France has departed, or is fast departing, from its favourite classical type, and adopting, though with unequal power, the broader and more natural lines of the Shakespearian model.

His practice is an example, his declarations are oracles.

Still, as I have said, the wide region of intellectual enjoyment over which our great bard exerts dominion, is not one parcelled out or divided into formal and state-like provinces. While the student of science is reading in his chamber the great "Principia" of Newton, he must keep before him the solution of only one problem. On that his mind must undistractedly rest, on that his power of thought be intensely concentrated. Woe to him if imagination leads his reason into truant wanderings; woe if he drop the thread of finely-drawn deductions! He will find his wearied intelligence drowsily floundering in a sea of swimming figures and evanescent quantities, or floating amidst the fragments of a shipwrecked diagram. But over Shakespeare one may dream no less than pore; we may drop the book from our hand and the contents remain equally before us. Stretched in the shade by a brook in summer, or sunk in the reading chair by the hearth in winter, in the imaginative vigour of health, in the drooping spirits of indisposition, one may read, and allow the trains of fancy which spring up in any scene to pursue their own way,

and minister their own varied pleasure or relief ; and
when by degrees we have become familiar with the
inexhaustible resources of his genius, there is scarcely
a want in mind or the affections that needs no higher
than human succour, which will not find in one or
other of his works that which will soothe suffering,
comfort grief, strengthen good desires, and present
some majestic example to copy, or some fearful
phantom. But when we endeavour to contemplate all his infinitely varied conceptions as
blended together in one picture, so as to take in,
if possible, at one glance the prodigious extent
of his prolific genius, we thereby build up what
he himself so beautifully called the " fabric of
a vision," matchless in its architecture, as in the
airiness of its materials. There are forms fantas-
tically sketched in cloud-shapes, such as *Hamlet*
showed to *Polonius*, in the midst of others rounded
and full, which open and unfold ever-changing
varieties, now gloomy and threatening, then
tipped with gold and tinted with azure, ever-
rolling, ever-moving, melting the one into the
other, or extricating each itself from the general
mass. Dwelling upon this maze of things and
imaginations, the most incongruous combinations

come before the dreamy thought, fascinated, spell-
bound, and entranced. The wild Ardennes and
Windsor Park seem to run into one another, their
firs and their oaks mingle together; the boisterous
ocean boiling round "the still vexed Bermoothes"
runs smoothly into the lagoons of Venice; the old
grey porticos of republican Rome, like the transi-
tion in a dissolving view, are confused and entangled
with the slim and fluted pillars of a Gothic hall;
here the golden orb, dropped from the hand of a
captive king, rolls on the ground side by side with
a jester's mouldy skull—both emblems of a common
fate in human things. Then the grave chief justice
seems incorporated in the bloated *Falstaff; King
John* and his barons are wassailing with *Poins*
and *Bardolph* at an inn door; *Coriolanus* and *Shylock* are contending for the right of human sensi-
bilities; *Macbeth* and *Jacques* are moralising
together on tenderness even to the brute. And so
of other more delicate creations of the poet's mind
—*Isabella* and *Ophelia, Desdemona* and the Scotch
Thane's wife produce respectively composite figures
of inextricable confusion. And around and above
is that filmy world, *Ariel* and *Titania* and *Peas-
blossom* and *Cobweb* and *Moth,* who weave us a

gossamer cloud around the vision, dimming it gradually before our eyes, in the last drooping of weariness, or the last hour of wakefulness.

*   *   *   *   *   *   *

APPENDIX.

PROPOSAL FOR A TERCENTENARY MEMORIAL OF SHAKESPEARE.

NEARLY one quarter of the year especially dedicated to the commemoration of our greatest Poet has passed away, without anything approaching to a practical determination on the mode of permanently celebrating it having been reached. London and Stratford-upon-Avon still hold contending claims, and it will be difficult to adjust them.

Nor can we consider passing and unenduring tributes to his memory and fame sufficient for marking so important an epoch. Speeches, oratorios, theatrical representations, and such other demonstrations of admiration, will end with the breath that utters them, leaving not a wrack behind, nor any vestige by which posterity may

be able to judge of our age's appreciation of Shakespeare, or of our power to give it any lasting expression.

Hence it seems agreed on all sides that a monument must be erected to him worthy of our time
and of his country ; such that, should art advance
or decline, it will at least show forth our love and
reverence for the Bard by proving that we did our
very best to honour him.

In our momentary or apparent embarrassment,
it can hardly be presumptuous to put forward a
new suggestion, not intended to interfere with this
idea, but designed to make it more complete.

And first let us assume that no monument, of
whatever form, that may be proposed and accepted,
can possibly be completed within the Shakespearian
year. If it have to be a mere statue, and no competition be permitted, no artist of any reputation
would undertake to prepare first his *bozzetto* to be
approved, then his model, and, lastly, his perennial
statue in marble or bronze, with its becoming pedestal, rich in relief, so that it could be set up
within the twelvemonth. Still less could this haste,
inconsistent with perfection, be used in a memorial
of a more complicated character, and involving the
concurrence of various arts. If fresco, for instance,

have to be employed, the architect must have
finished his work thoroughly before the painter can
commence.

These preliminary remarks are here introduced
to anticipate and disarm any objections, on the
score of required time, to the proposal about to
be submitted to public judgment.

We will now ask leave to make some observations on the characteristics which a monument
worthy of its proposed object should present.

First, if possible, it should not be altogether
local. A monument fixed and permanent in one
only place necessarily offers limited enjoyment and
improvement only to a few. Stratford does not
lie in the line of general circulation ; and if the
house and tomb of the great Poet attract compara-
tively but few pilgrims, we can hardly expect a
greater confluence of them to visit a modern memorial. London, on the other hand, is too vast
for any one centre to collect its inhabitants ;
while the many who travel to it from afar have
generally occupations or engagements of a different
character from the curiosity or devotion that would
lead them to any point of the metropolis for the
purpose of seeing Shakespeare's Tercentenary
Monument. And, seen once, it would be scarcely

F

ever revisited. It may, therefore, be worth while
to consider whether such a memorial, connected
most specially with the present year, could not be
devised as would be within the reach of many,
which the merchant of Liverpool and Manchester,
or the educated country gentleman who seldom
brings his family to London, could enjoy, and
transmit to his children as a valuable demonstra-
tion of what England could do, and did, for the
greatest of her authors in 1864.

Further, it may be observed that a mere statue
or other sculptured monument will employ not
only few men who give lustre to the period, but
will necessarily present to futurity only an inade-
quate means of ascertaining what many would be
willing to do in order to hand down their names
as tributaries to that genius who can better inspire
them than any other native writer, if scope were
given them to bring the immense resources of art
possessed by the age and country to converge
on one point—the leaving a memorial of him
worthy both of the commemorators and of the
commemorated.

In other words, the monument should not be
partial or limited, but embrace and transmit to
after-ages a fair exhibition of many combined

powers, never before united to honour any one else.

But still more, we must not forget that Shakespeare's character and merits belong essentially to our literature. A *literary* monument seems therefore naturally called for ; or at any rate literature should be the groundwork of anything done to celebrate the name highest in its ranks.

Now, who will venture to do for Shakespeare what he has done for himself? He may indeed . say, what Horace did, that he has erected " a monument more enduring than brass," that in his day " he accomplished a work which neither the elements in their fury, nor fire, nor hostile steel, nor consuming time will ever destroy." Yet, whatever is so far proposed to be done cannot be more lasting than bronze, nor exempt from these destructive agencies. Let our monument partake of the imperishableness which the poet has gained ; and let all our puny efforts go no further than to add grace and give increased honour to him and his works.

The simple and obvious way of meeting these requisites and conditions seems to be—

The publication of such an edition of Shake-

speare's complete works as in its text, its typo-
graphy, and its illustration should be unrivalled.

Let us offer a few more detailed remarks on this
proposal.

I. THE TEXT. The selection of the purest text
must be entrusted to a small committee or sub-
committee of Shakespearian scholars of acknowledged pre-eminence ; and this should be so chosen
and edited as to form, for ever, the admitted
standard of the Poet's works.

It should be printed without notes, beyond any
various reading of real consequence and weight, at
the foot of the page. A short "argument" may
be prefixed to each drama ; though, as the edition
would not be intended for learners, this might be
dispensed with.

An entire volume might contain a glossary in
alphabetical order for the whole of Shakespeare's
works ; and an "apparatus," as it used to be
called, comprising a carefully prepared catalogue
of editions, and of every work, book, pamphlet, or
paper, that has ever appeared, at home or abroad,
on his writings. Whatever is known of his life,
and all remaining memorials of him, would find a
place in this supplementary volume.

We need hardly add that this edition would include the sonnets, and any other compositions connected with Shakespeare's name.

II. THE TYPOGRAPHY. It would be presumptuous in us to suggest anything on this head, further than to express a hope, or rather an assurance, that this great requisite for carrying out our proposal would be undertaken by one or more of those great masters in the art of printing who abound in England, and have already produced works which place the press of this country on a level, at least, with that of any other. In type, in paper, in perfection of press-work, it would go hard with us indeed if we could not bring forward in honour of Shakespeare such a specimen of typographical skill and taste as has never yet been witnessed. We feel sure that it would be accepted by the present generation, and treasured by ages to come, as the unrivalled production of the press, rising as superior to every previous effort as the author whom it perpetuates is to all other writers in our language.

And that it will probably never be reached in times to come may be secured by the union, in this publication, of abilities not easily brought together, except by such a grand national undertaking. To this great point we proceed.

III. THE ILLUSTRATIONS. These we will classify under four distinct heads.

1. To each play should be prefixed an engraving of an appropriate sketch, expressly drawn by some artist of the highest class and of acknowledged reputation. Thirty-two or thirty-four will be required; and we may hope that, without requiring duplicates from any one, the United Kingdom can furnish artists equal to their production. It need not be said that these drawings should be of exquisite finish, works of love, worthy of their intention, and of the place they are destined to hold in connection with the greatest name in our literature.

Naturally a scene would be chosen for each subject which would suggest a perfect and characteristic composition; and which of Shakespeare's dramas contains not one such at least, in a true artist's estimation? Indeed, much has already been done in preparation for such an application of British art. Our annual exhibitions seldom fail to present to us subjects taken from our national Bard. We have seen "Hamlet with the Players," "Wolsey at the Abbey-Gate," "Ophelia floating on the Stream," "Malvolio," "Puck," and fifty other characters have given subjects to smaller paintings. Nor must we forget "King Lear and his Daughters" among the frescoes of our greatest public building.

But these greater illustrations need not be necessarily historical; every branch of art may find its place. Will not the "beeches and ferns" of England be characteristic of Windsor Forest, better than a mere scene in its play? And have we not an artist from whom "The Tempest" would receive a pictorial description worthy to stand side by side with Shakespeare's text?

Perhaps the great difficulty to be here encountered is in the engraving of such works. For they must not be entrusted to xylography; and, before evanescent photography has driven the immortalizing graver from the field of art, let us in this work leave to posterity a specimen of our prowess on copper or steel.

From the purest line-engraving to the more popular and more complicated, though less artistic, processes by which so much effect is produced in modern calchography, let us put on record for ever what the art of Marc Antonio could do in

England in 1864. The style of each artist will naturally suggest that of its engraving.

2. Each act, if possible, should have in the middle of the page one polychrome picture, such as adorn so admirably Mr. James Doyle's "Annals," in which the costumes, arms, furniture, dwellings, architecture of the piece, with the arts and customs of its place and time, may be accurately represented. From these smaller illustrations the play ought to be able to be acted by any persons wishing to be exact in scenery and costume in any country.

3. The perfection to which art has arrived in colour-printing would enable us to complete our illustrations by borders such as have never before been produced. It would enable many artists who represent amongst us decorative art, illumination, and arabesque, once so highly prized, to contribute their share towards this intended work, and add to its singular beauty.

Each play would have its own border, decorating two pages, or an open leaf, in colour.

Now, it is one of the great gifts and glories of Shakespeare to have touched with his wand of light every period of civilized art, from the early dawn of literature to his own time. To record this universality of connection between his writings and art, it is proposed that the borders should commemorate the character of art flourishing in the country and period to which the drama belongs.— We will make a rough outline of the connections which would result.

Artistic periods.	Plays.
ARCHAIC GREEK AND ASIATIC (*Ægina and Lycian Marbles*),	Troilus and Cressida.
CLASSICAL GREEK,	Comedy of Errors—Timon.
ETRUSCAN (*Corioli and ancient Rome*),	Coriolanus.
CLASSICAL ROMAN (*Baths of Titus, &c.*),	Julius Cæsar.
EGYPTIAN,	Antony and Cleopatra.
CELTIC (*interlacing, as in Irish*),	King Lear—Cymbeline.
SCANDINAVIAN,	Hamlet.
MEDIÆVAL ENGLISH (*MSS.*),	John *to* Richard III.
SCOTCH,	Macbeth.
FRENCH,	All's Well that Ends Well.
SPANISH,	Love's Labour Lost.
RENAISSANCE (*Loggie, Giulio Clovio, &c.*),	Henry VIII.
ITALIAN CINQUECENTO,	Two Gentlemen of Verona, Taming of the Shrew, Romeo and Juliet.
VENETIAN,	Othello—Merchant of Venice.

The whole history of decorative art, which may

be called the history of taste, would thus be associated from its dawn to the commencement of its decay with our great Bard. He will be shown to have sung of whatever in time or place was worthy of his genius. Sometimes solid monuments, like "the Stones of Venice," will have to guide the artist's pencil; but often, as in the matchless series of English historical plays, our own manuscripts, with their splendid illuminations, will give a complete course of our decorative art.

And after historical decoration shall have been thus exhausted, there will still remain six or seven plays, unattached, so to speak, in which would be room for the Flora, the Fauna, and the Fairydom of Shakespeare to disport round the margins of his ample page under the luxurious but judicious guidance of poetical artists.

4. There would still remain occupation for wood-engraving, in titles, initial letters, and tail-pieces, analogous to the subjects of the plays.

Naturally the binding will be made to recall the periods when the taste and beauty of the outward covering gave earnest of the splendour which it protected.

IV. The Management of this Proposal. There

is not the slightest idea of proposing any interfer-
ence with the existing Centenary Committee, which
includes in itself probably all, at any rate most, of
the persons best capable of carrying this scheme
into successful execution.

All that would be required from it would be a
delegation of some of its functions to sub-com-
mittees, which would work harmoniously together,
settle the details of what is here presented only in
block, obtain co-operation, distribute the work, and
set it a-going. But the groundwork of such sub-
committees exists, and may easily be built on.
Probably, in any other country, no small part
would have been allotted, in what the country
wished to do, to such societies as have a national
character and representation for such undertakings.
In England too, had science been in question—
had it been proposed to erect a memorial to
Newton, still more, had it been suggested to combine with it a perfect edition of his works, no one
can doubt that the leaders in such a movement
would have been the great scientific Societies, such
as the Royal and the Astronomical.

And here, why should not the established, and
now recognized, Committee for the Shakespeare
Memorial call in the assistance of such Societies as

that of Literature, or the Philological, for the text, and of the Royal Academy for the illustration, of the work that has been described? These bodies could not, indeed, act corporately, but they could depute a certain number of persons to represent them, active and able, as well as willing, to devote themselves to the undertaking; and either belonging to them already, or easily created honorary members.

Such a compound, not over-numerous, committee once formed, would suggest, without jealousy, the addition of other representative members; for example, from the Universities, from the British Museum, and from other learned associations in London and in other cities.*

V. We will throw into our concluding section a few miscellaneous observations.

1. It might seem selfish to confine our tribute to Shakespeare to the efforts and contributions of our own country. We should not refuse advice or offers of assistance from abroad. Should we find an insufficiency of artists willing to give a helping hand at home, we feel sure that the land of Schlegel and of Schiller, of the critics and poets who have

* As the Arundel, the Surtees, &c.

so thoroughly appreciated our Bard, would be as
ready to illustrate his beauties with the pencil as it
has been with the pen. The schools of Munich and
of Berlin, of Vienna and Düsseldorf, could furnish
men who would not refuse to assist us if necessary.

But, though we feel sure on this point, would it
not be a gracious offer to make to any of these
great schools, that it would undertake the entire
illustration, on the plan adopted, of some one play,
congenial to German taste and character?

2. The proposed plan will, no doubt, be expen-
sive, for though, doubtless, the noble and patriotic
feelings of many artists will impel them to work
for the national glory and their admiration of
Shakespeare, much must be adequately remune-
rated; and the mechanical labour cannot be
obtained free-cost. But the scheme ought to be
remunerative. No one, who is able, will grudge a
subscription, which, being spread over several
years, will give a return, in the shape of an unequalled Memorial of the Tercentenary Commemoration of our Poet, one portable, personal, and at
all times accessible. Let due calculations be made
for something magnificent, if you please; then add
margin enough to help or originate other purposes.

3. For instance, we cannot but fear that the

attempt to provide a monument out of the common line of such memorials may fail from many causes. A statue of Shakespeare must represent Shakespeare, and nothing more. He is too familiar to us as himself to be idealized, attitudinized, or thrown into raptures. The noble, well-known face must be before us; and there must be no startling, or allegorical, still less mythological, accompaniments. All this reduces a sculptured monument to a small compass. If erected in a vast open space, you must either make it colossal, or it will dwindle down to disproportion. Let the Achilles, in the Park, be a warning to us not to attempt the gigantic.

It has struck us that the most suitable site for a statue of Shakespeare should combine several conditions easily attainable. It should be in a central position, among his people, and daily visible without effort, especially by those whose very occupation is to honour him and recognize his merits. It should be amidst buildings that can give it right proportions even to unpractised eyes, which have no scale of dimensions without the familiar measures of ordinary objects. It should be placed where these objects would be in natural correlation with him whom it represents.

Such a site, it appears to us, is to be found in the area in front of the British Museum, our only and noble temple of our literature and of ancient art. A statue in bronze, of large proportions, placed on a noble pedestal, adorned with two inscriptions in English and in Latin, and two relievos representing in some way the character of his unrivalled genius, would, if placed there, be visible all day and every day, to every passer-by, without jealous guardianship; would be saluted by every student as he passed on to pursue his own studies, and by the tens of thousands who yearly visit the Galleries, and would be, where it should be, at the very gate of that realm over which the memory of Shakespeare reigns supreme.

4. Indeed, it would show the way to that real Memorial of himself, which the Poet has raised, and which, in its most perfect and precious form, would be preserved within.

For we would finally suggest that two copies of the proposed edition of Shakespeare's works should be printed on vellum.

One should have incorporated in it all the original drawings, plain or coloured, furnished by the artists of every class for its embellishment. Thus posterity would be able to see, not in transcripts, however accurate, but in the very pencil-strokes of the artist, the character and perfection of his work.

The second copy the committee would naturally offer as a worthy tribute to the Sovereign whose reign has been especially graced by the occurrence in, we may hope, its yet long duration, of the Tercentenary Commemoration of England's first literary Son.

N. CARD. WISEMAN.

London, March 22*nd,* 1864.

THE END.

LONDON: PRINTED BY MACDONALD AND TUOWELL, BLENHEIM HOUSE.

13, GREAT MARLBOROUGH STREET.

MESSRS. HURST AND BLACKETT'S LIST OF NEW WORKS.

A JOURNEY FROM LONDON TO PERSE-
POLIS; including WANDERINGS IN DAGHESTAN, GEORGIA,
ARMENIA, KURDISTAN, MESOPOTAMIA, AND PERSIA.
By J. USSHER, Esq., F.R.G.S. Royal 8vo, with numerous beautiful
Coloured Illustrations. 42s. Elegantly bound.

"This work does not yield to any recent book of travels in extent and variety of
interest. Its title, 'From London to Persepolis,' is well chosen and highly sugges-
tive. A wonderful chain of association is suspended from these two points, and the
traveller goes along its line, gathering link after link into his hand, each gemmed
with thought, knowledge, speculation, and adventure. The reader will feel that
in closing this memorable book he takes leave of a treasury of knowledge. The
whole book is interesting, and its unaffected style and quick spirit of observation
lend an unfailing freshness to its pages. The illustrations are beautiful, and have
been executed with admirable taste and judgment."—*Post.*

"This work is in every way creditable to the author, who has produced a mass
of pleasant reading, both entertaining and instructive. Mr. Ussher's journey may
be defined as a complete oriental grand tour of the Asiatic west-central district.
He started down the Danube, making for Odessa. Thence, having duly 'done' the
Crimea, he coasted the Circassian shore in a steamer to Poti, and from that to
Tiflis. This was the height of summer, and, the season being favourable, he crossed
the Dariel Pass northwards, turned to the east, and visited the mountain fastnesses
of Shamil's country, recently conquered by the Russians. Thence he returned to
Tiflis by the old Persian province of Shirvan, along the Caspian, by Derbend and
the famous fire-springs of Baku. From Tiflis he went to Gumri, and over the
frontier to Kars, and the splendid ruins of Ani, and through the Russian territory
to the Turkish frontier fortress of Bayazid, stopping by the way at Erivan and the
great monastery of Etchmiadzin. From Bayazid he went to Van, and saw all the
chief points of interest on the lake of that name; thence to Bitlis and Diarbekir.
From Diarbekir he went to Mosul by the upper road, visited Nineveh, paid his
respects to the winged bulls and all our old friends there, and floated on his raft of
inflated skins down the Tigris to Baghdad. From Mosul he made an excursion to
the devil-worshipping country, and another from Baghdad to Hilleh and the Birs
Nimrud, or so-called Tower of Babel. After resting in the city of the Caliphs, he
followed the track of his illustrious predecessor, Sindbad, only on board
of a different craft, having got a passage in the steamer Comet; and the English
mouthly sailing packet took him from Bassora across the gulf to Bushire. From
thence he went to Tehran over the 'broad dominions of the king of kings,' stopping
at all the interesting places, particularly at Persepolis; and from Tehran returned
home through Armenia by Trebisonde and the Black Sea."—*Saturday Review.*

"This is a book of travel of which no review can give an adequate idea. The
extent of country traversed, the number and beauty of the coloured illustrations,
and the good sense, humour, and information with which it abounds, all tend to
increase the author's just meed of praise, while they render the critic's task all the
harder. We must, after all, trust to our readers to explore for themselves the many
points of amusement, interest and beauty which the book contains. We can assure
them that they will not meet with a single page of dulness. Mr. Ussher handles
such topics as Persepolis, Nineveh, and the cities of the Eastern world, with singular completeness, and leaves the ordinary reader nothing to desire. The coloured
illustrations are really perfect of their kind. Merely as a collection of spirited, well-
coloured engravings they are worth the cost of the whole volume."—*Herald.*

"Mr. Ussher went by the Danube to Constantinople, crossed thence to Sebastopol,
and passed through the Crimea to Kertch, and so on to Poti. From Poti he went
to Tetlis, and made thence an excursion to Gunib and Baku on the Caspian. The
record of this journey is the most interesting part of the book. Having returned to
Tetlis, Mr. Ussher visited Gumri and Kars, and went thence to Lake Van, and so by
Diarbekr and Mosul to Baghdad. From Baghdad he went to Babylon and Kerbela,
and returning to Baghdad, descended the river to Basra, and crossed to Bushire.
Thence he went by Shiraz and Isfahan to Tehran, and returned to Europe by the
Tabreez and Trebisonde route. The reader will find the author of this pleasant
volume an agreeable companion. He is a good observer, and describes well what
he sees."—*Athenæum.*

"A truly magnificent work, adorned with gorgeously-coloured illustrations. We
are lured over its pages with a pleasant fascination, and derive no little information
from so agreeable a cicerone as Mr. Ussher."—*Sun.*

MESSRS. HURST AND BLACKETT'S
NEW WORKS—*Continued.*

COURT AND SOCIETY FROM ELIZABETH

TO ANNE, Edited from the Papers at Kimbolton, by the DUKE OF MANCHESTER. *Second Edition, Revised.* 2 vols. 8vo, with Fine Portraits. 30s., bound.

"The Duke of Manchester has done a welcome service to the lover of gossip and secret history by publishing these family papers. Persons who like to see greatness without the plumes and mail in which history presents it, will accept these volumes with hearty thanks to their noble editor. In them will be found something new about many men and women in whom the reader can never cease to feel an interest—much about the divorce of Henry the Eighth and Catherine of Arragon—a great deal about the love affairs of Queen Elizabeth—something about Bacon, and (indirectly) about Shakspeare—more about Lord Essex and Lady Rich—the very strange story of Walter Montagu, poet, profligate, courtier, pervert, secret agent, abbot —many details of the Civil War and Cromwell's Government, and of the Restoration— much that is new about the Revolution and the Settlement, the exiled Court of St. Germains, the wars of William of Orange, the campaigns of Marlborough, the intrigues of Duchess Sarah, and the town life of fine ladies and gentlemen during the days of Anne. With all this is mingled a good deal of gossip about the loves of great poets, the frailties of great beauties, the rivalries of great wits, the quarrels of great peers."—*Athenæum.*

"These volumes are sure to excite curiosity. A great deal of interesting matter is here collected, from sources which are not within everybody's reach."—*Times.*

"The public are indebted to the noble author for contributing, from the archives of his ancestral seat, many important documents otherwise inaccessible to the historical inquirer, as well as for the lively, picturesque, and piquant sketches of Court and Society, which render his work powerfully attractive to the general reader. The work contains varied information relating to secret Court intrigues, numerous narratives of an exciting nature, and valuable materials for authentic history. Scarcely any personage whose name figured before the world during the long period embraced by the volumes is passed over in silence."—*Morning Post.*

THE LIFE OF THE REV. EDWARD IRVING,

Minister of the National Scotch Church, London. Illustrated by his Journal and Correspondence. By Mrs. OLIPHANT. *Fourth and Cheaper Edition, Revised,* in 1 vol., with Portrait, 5s., bound.

"We who read these memoirs must own to the nobility of Irving's character, the grandeur of his aims, and the extent of his powers. His friend Carlyle bears this testimony to his worth:—'I call him, on the whole, the best man I have ever, after trial enough, found in this world, or hope to find.' A character such as this is deserving of study, and his life ought to be written. Mrs. Oliphant has undertaken the work and has produced a biography of considerable merit. The author fully understands her hero, and sets forth the incidents of his career with the skill of a practised hand. The book is a good book on a most interesting theme."—*Times.*

"Mrs. Oliphant's 'Life of Edward Irving' supplies a long-felt desideratum. It is copious, earnest, and eloquent. On every page there is the impress of a large and masterly comprehension, and of a bold, fluent, and poetic skill of portraiture. Irving as a man and as a pastor is not only fully sketched, but exhibited with many broad, powerful, and life-like touches, which leave a strong impression."—*Edinburgh Review.*

"A truly interesting and most affecting memoir. Irving's life ought to have a niche in every gallery of religious biography. There are few lives that will be fuller of instruction, interest, and consolation."—*Saturday Review.*

THE LIFE OF JOSIAH WEDGWOOD. From

his Private Correspondence and Family Papers, in the possession of JOSEPH MAYER, Esq., F.S.A., FRANCIS WEDGWOOD, Esq., C. DARWIN, Esq., M.A., F.S.A., &c., and other Original Sources. By ELIZA METEYARD. 2 vols. 8vo, with fine Portraits and other Illustrations. (In the Press.)

MESSRS. HURST AND BLACKETT'S NEW WORKS—*Continued.*

MY LIFE AND RECOLLECTIONS. By the HON. GRANTLEY F. BERKELEY. 2 vols. 8vo, with Portrait. 30s.

Among the other distinguished persons mentioned in this work are:—Kings George III. and IV., and William IV.; Queens Charlotte, Caroline, and Victoria; the Prince of Wales; the Dukes of Kent, Cumberland, Sussex, Cambridge, d'Aumale, Wellington, Norfolk, Richmond, Beaufort, Bedford, Devonshire, St. Albans, Manchester, Portland; the Marquises of Anglesea, Buckingham, Downshire, Waterford, Tavistock, Londonderry, Clanricarde, Breadalbane, Worcester; Lords Mulgrave, Conynham, Clanwilliam, Wynford, Palmerston, Bathurst, Cantelupe, Roden, Eldon, Grey, Holland, Coleraine, Rokeby, Munster, Chelmsford, Ducie, Alvanley, Chesterfield, Sefton, Derby, Vane, Mexborough, George Bentinck, Edward Somerset, Fitzclarence, Egremont, Count d'Orsay; the Bishop of Oxford, Cardinal Wiseman; Sirs Lumley Skeffington, William Wynn, Percy Shelley, Godfrey Webster, Samuel Romilly, Matthew Tierney, Francis Burdett; Messrs. Fox, Sheridan, Whitbread, Brummell, Byng, Townsend, Bernal, Maginn, Cobden, Bright, O'Connell, Crockford, &c.; the Duchesses of Devonshire, Gordon, Rutland, Argyle; Ladies Clermont, Berkeley, Shelley, Guest, Fitzhardinge, Bury, Blessington, Craven, Essex, Strangford, Paget; Mesdames Fitzherbert, Coutts, Jordan, Billington, Mardyn, Shelley, Misses Landon, Kemble, Paton, &c.

"A book unrivalled in its position in the range of modern literature."—*Times.*

"There is a large fund of amusement in these volumes. The details of the author's life are replete with much that is interesting. A book so brimful of anecdote cannot but be successful."—*Athenæum.*

"This work contains a great deal of amusing matter; and that it will create a sensation no one can doubt. Mr. Berkeley can write delightfully when he pleases. His volumes will, of course, be extensively read, and, as a literary venture, may be pronounced a success."—*Post.*

"A clever, freespoken man of the world, son of an earl with £70,000 a-year, who has lived from boyhood the life of a club-man, sportsman, and man of fashion, has thrown his best stories about himself and his friends into an anecdotic autobiography. Of course it is eminently readable. Mr. Grantley Berkeley writes easily and well. The book is full of pleasant stories, all told as easily and clearly as if they were related at a club-window, and all with point of greater or less piquancy."—*Spectator.*

HAUNTED LONDON. By WALTER THORNBURY. 1 vol. 8vo, with numerous Illustrations by F. W. FAIRHOLT, F.S.A. 21s., elegantly bound.

"Haunted London is a pleasant book."—*Ath næum.*

"Pleasant reading is Mr. Thornbury's 'Haunted London'—a gossiping, historical, antiquarian, topographical volume, amusing both to the Londoner and the country cousin."—*Star.*

"Mr. Thornbury points out to us the legendary houses, the great men's birthplaces and tombs, the haunts of poets, the scenes of martyrdom, the battle-fields of old factions. The book overflows with anecdotical gossip. Mr. Fairholt's drawings add alike to its value and interest."—*Notes and Queries.*

"As pleasant a book as well could be, forming a very handsome volume—a volume worthy of being pronounced an acquisition either for the table or the bookshelf. A capital title is 'Haunted London'—meaning by that not merely localities like Cock Lane, but all London. For is it not haunted, this London of ours? Haunted happily, by ghosts of memories that will not be laid. What footsteps have not traversed these causeways, inhabited these dwelling-houses, prayed in these churches, wept in these graveyards, laughed in these theatres? And of all these Mr. Thornbury discourses—shrewdly, like an observant man of the world; gracefully, like a skilled man of letters; lovingly, like a sympathizing fellow-creature; courtier and playwright, student and actress, statesman and mountebank, he has an eye for them all. Saunter with him down any street he may seem fain to conduct you through, and before you get to the end of it we wager you will be wiser than at starting—certainly, beyond any doubt of it, you will have been entertained."—*Sun.*

MESSRS. HURST AND BLACKETT'S
NEW WORKS—*Continued.*

A PERSONAL NARRATIVE OF THIRTEEN
YEARS' SERVICE AMONGST THE WILD TRIBES OF KHONDISTAN, FOR THE SUPPRESSION OF HUMAN SACRIFICE. By Major-General JOHN CAMPBELL, C.B. 1 vol. 8vo, with Illustrations.

"Major-General Campbell's book is one of thrilling interest, and must be pronounced the most remarkable narrative of the present season."—*Athenæum.*

THE DESTINY OF NATIONS, AS INDICATED
IN PROPHECY. By the Rev. JOHN CUMMING, D.D. 1 vol. 7s. 6d.

"Among the subjects expounded by Dr. Cumming in this interesting volume are The Little Horn, or The Papacy; The Waning Crescent, Turkey; The Lost Ten Tribes; and the Future of the Jews and Judea, Africa, France, Russia, America, Great Britain, &c."—*Observer.* "One of the most able of Dr. Cumming's works."—*Messenger.*

MEMOIRS OF JANE CAMERON, FEMALE
CONVICT. By a Prison Matron, Author of "Female Life in Prison." 2 vols. 21s.

"This narrative, as we can well believe, is truthful in every important particular—a faithful chronicle of a woman's fall and rescue. It is a book that ought to be widely read."—*Examiner.* "There can be no doubt as to the interest of the book, which, moreover, is very well written."—*Athenæum.*

"Once or twice a-year one rises from reading a book with a sense of real gratitude to the author, and this book is one of these. There are many ways in which it has a rare value. The artistic touches in this book are worthy of De Foe."—*Reader.*

TRAVELS AND ADVENTURES OF AN OFFI-
CER'S WIFE IN INDIA, CHINA, AND NEW ZEALAND. By Mrs. MUTER, Wife of Lieut.-Colonel D. D. MUTER, 13th (Prince Albert's) Light Infantry. 2 vols. 21s.

"Mrs. Muter's travels deserve to be recommended, as combining instruction and amusement in a more than ordinary degree. The work has the interest of a romance added to that of history."—*Athenæum.*

TRAVELS ON HORSEBACK IN MANTCHU
TARTARY: being a Summer's Ride beyond the Great Wall of China. By GEORGE FLEMING, Military Train. 1 vol. royal 8vo, with Map and 50 Illustrations.

"Mr. Fleming's narrative is a most charming one. He has an untrodden region to tell of, and he photographs it and its people and their ways. Life-like descriptions are interspersed with personal anecdotes, local legends, and stories of adventure, some of them revealing no common artistic power."—*Spectator.*

HISTORY OF ENGLAND, FROM THE
ACCESSION OF JAMES I. TO THE DISGRACE OF CHIEF JUSTICE COKE. By SAMUEL RAWSON GARDINER. 2 vols. 8vo.

ADVENTURES AND RESEARCHES among the
ANDAMAN ISLANDERS. By Dr. MOUAT, F.R.G.S., &c 1 vol. demy 8vo, with Illustrations.

"Dr. Mouat's book, whilst forming a most important and valuable contribution to ethnology, will be read with interest by the general reader."—*Athenæum.*

MEMOIRS OF QUEEN HORTENSE, MOTHER
OF NAPOLEON III. Cheaper Edition, in 1 vol. 6s.

"A biography of the beautiful and unhappy Queen, more satisfactory than any we have yet met with."—*Daily News.*

MESSRS. HURST AND BLACKETT'S
NEW WORKS—*Continued.*

REMINISCENCES OF THE OPERA. By BEN-
JAMIN LUMLEY, Twenty Years Director of Her Majesty's Theatre.
8vo, with Portrait of the Author by Count D'Orsay. 16s.

"Mr. Lumley's book, with all its sparkling episodes, is really a well-digested history of an institution of social importance in its time, interspersed with sound opinions and shrewd and mature reflections."—*Times.*

"As a repertory of anecdote, we have not for a long while met with anything at all comparable to these unusually brilliant and most diversified Reminiscences. They reveal the Twenty Years' Director of Her Majesty's Theatre to us in the thick and throng of all his radiant associations. They take us luringly—as it were, led by the button-hole—behind the scenes, in every sense of that decoying and profoundly attractive phrase. They introduce us to all the stars—now singly, now in very constellations. They bring us rapidly, delightfully, and exhilaratingly to a knowledge so intimate of what has really been doing there in the Realm of Song, not only behind the scenes and in the green-room, but in the reception-apartment of the Director himself, that we are *au courant* with all the whims and oddities of the strange world in which he fills so high and responsible a position. Reading Mr. Lumley, we now know more than we have ever known before of such Queens of the Lyric stage as Pasta, Catalini, Malibran, Grisi, Sontag, and Piccolomini—of such light-footed fairies of the ballet as Taglioni, Fanny Ellsler, and Cerito—of such primi tenori as Rubini, Mario, Gardoni, and Giuglini—of such baritones as Ronconi and Tamburini—or of such bassi profondi as the wondrous Staudigl and the mighty Lablache. Nay, Mr. Lumley takes us out of the glare of the footlights, away from the clang of the orchestra, into the dream-haunted presence of the great composers of the age, bringing us face to face, as it were, among others, with Rossini, Mendelssohn, Meyerbeer, Verdi, Balfe, and Donizetti. He lets us into the mysteries of his correspondence—now with Count Cavour, now with Prince Metternich—for, in his doings, in his movements, in his negotiations, Sovereigns, Prime Ministers, Ambassadors, and Governments are, turn by turn, not merely courteously, but directly and profoundly interested! Altogether, Mr. Lumley's book is an enthralling one. It is written with sparkling vivacity, and is delightfully interesting throughout."—*Sun.*

"Everyone ought to read Mr. Lumley's very attractive 'Reminiscences of the Opera.' In the fashionable, dramatic, and literary worlds its cordial welcome is assured. It is a most entertaining volume. Anecdote succeeds to anecdote in this pleasant book with delightful fluency."—*Post.*

WILLIAM SHAKESPEARE. By VICTOR HUGO.
Authorized English Translation. 1 vol. 8vo, 12s.

"M. Victor Hugo has produced a notable and brilliant book about Shakespeare. M. Hugo sketches the life of Shakespeare, and makes of it a very effective picture. Imagination and pleasant fancy are mingled with the facts. There is high colouring, but therewith a charm which has not hitherto been found in any portrait of Shakespeare painted by a foreign hand. The biographical details are manipulated by a master's hand, and consequently there is an agreeable air of novelty even about the best known circumstances."—*Athenæum.*

LIFE IN JAVA; WITH SKETCHES OF THE
JAVANESE. By WILLIAM BARRINGTON D'ALMEIDA. 2 vols. post
8vo, with Illustrations. 21s., bound.

"'Life in Java' is both amusing and instructive. The author saw a good deal of the country and people not generally known."—*Athenæum.*
"Mr. D'Almeida's volumes traverse interesting ground. They are filled with good and entertaining matter."—*Examiner.*
"A very entertaining work. The author has given most interesting pictures of the country and the people. There are not many authentic works on Java, and these volumes will rank among the best."—*Post.*

A LADY'S VISIT TO MANILLA AND JAPAN.
By ANNA D'A. 1 vol., with Illustrations.

"This book is written in a lively, agreeable, natural style, and we cordially recommend it as containing a fund of varied information connected with the Far East, not to be found recorded in so agreeable a manner in any other volume with which we are acquainted."—*Press.*

13, Great Marlborough Street.

MESSRS. HURST AND BLACKETT'S
NEW WORKS—*Continued.*

THE WANDERER IN WESTERN FRANCE.
By G. T. Lowth, Esq., Author of "The Wanderer in Arabia." Illustrated by the Hon. Eliot Yorke, M.P. 8vo.

A WINTER IN UPPER AND LOWER EGYPT.
By G. A. Hoskins, Esq., F.R.G.S. 1 vol., with Illustrations.

POINTS OF CONTACT BETWEEN SCIENCE AND ART.
By His Eminence Cardinal Wiseman. 8vo. 5s.

GREECE AND THE GREEKS.
Being the Narrative of a Winter Residence and Summer Travel in Greece and its Islands. By Fredrika Bremer. Translated by Mary Howitt. 2 vols.

MEMOIRS OF CHRISTINA, QUEEN OF SWEDEN.
By Henry Woodhead. 2 vols., with Portrait.

ENGLISH WOMEN OF LETTERS.
By Julia Kavanagh, Author of "Nathalie," "Adele," "French Women of Letters," "Beatrice," &c. 2 vols.

THE OKAVANGO RIVER: A NARRATIVE
OF TRAVEL, EXPLORATION, AND ADVENTURE. By C. J. Andersson, Author of "Lake Ngami." 1 vol., with Portrait and numerous Illustrations.

TRAVELS IN THE REGIONS OF THE AMOOR,
AND THE RUSSIAN ACQUISITIONS ON THE CONFINES OF INDIA AND CHINA. By T. W. Atkinson, F.G.S., F.R.G.S., Author of "Oriental and Western Siberia." Dedicated, by permission, to Her Majesty. Second Edition. Royal 8vo, with Map and 83 Illustrations, elegantly bound.

ITALY UNDER VICTOR EMMANUEL.
A Personal Narrative. By Count Charles Arrivabene. 2 vols. 8vo.

THE LIFE OF J. M. W. TURNER, R.A.,
from Original Letters and Papers furnished by his Friends and Fellow Academicians. By Walter Thornbury. 2 vols. 8vo, with Portraits and other Illustrations.

THE CHURCH AND THE CHURCHES;
or, THE PAPACY AND THE TEMPORAL POWER. By Dr. Döllinger. Translated by W. B. Mac Cabe. 8vo.

CHEAP EDITION of LES MISÉRABLES.
By Victor Hugo. The Authorized Copyright English Translation, Illustrated by Millais. 5s., bound.

"We think it will be seen on the whole that this work has something more than the beauties of an exquisite style or the word-compelling power of a literary Zeus to recommend it to the tender care of a distant posterity; that in dealing with all the emotions, passions, doubts, fears, which go to make up our common humanity, M. Victor Hugo has stamped upon every page the hall mark of genius and the loving patience and conscientious labour of a true artist. But the merits of 'Les Misérables' do not merely consist in the conception of it as a whole, it abounds page after page with details of unequalled beauty."—*Quarterly Review.*

Published annually, in One Vol., royal 8vo, with the Arms beautifully engraved, handsomely bound, with gilt edges, price 31s. 6d.

LODGE'S PEERAGE
AND BARONETAGE,
CORRECTED BY THE NOBILITY.

THE THIRTY-FOURTH EDITION FOR 1865 IS NOW READY.

LODGE'S PEERAGE AND BARONETAGE is acknowledged to be the most complete, as well as the most elegant, work of the kind. As an established and authentic authority on all questions respecting the family histories, honours, and connections of the titled aristocracy, no work has over stood so high. It is published under the especial patronage of Her Majesty, and is annually corrected throughout, from the personal communications of the Nobility. It is the only work of its class in which, *the type being kept constantly standing*, every correction is made in its proper place to the date of publication, an advantage which gives it supremacy over all its competitors. Independently of its full and authentic information respecting the existing Peers and Baronets of the realm, the most sedulous attention is given in its pages to the collateral branches of the various noble families, and the names of many thousand individuals are introduced, which do not appear in other records of the titled classes. For its authority, correctness, and facility of arrangement, and the beauty of its typography and binding, the work is justly entitled to the place it occupies on the tables of Her Majesty and the Nobility.

LIST OF THE PRINCIPAL CONTENTS.

Historical View of the Peerage.
Parliamentary Roll of the House of Lords.
English, Scotch, and Irish Peers, in their orders of Precedence.
Alphabetical List of Peers of Great Britain and the United Kingdom, holding superior rank in the Scotch or Irish Peerage.
Alphabetical list of Scotch and Irish Peers, holding superior titles in the Peerage of Great Britain and the United Kingdom.
A Collective list of Peers, in their order of Precedence.
Table of Precedency among Men.
Table of Precedency among Women.
The Queen and the Royal Family.
Peers of the Blood Royal.
The Peerage, alphabetically arranged.
Families of such Extinct Peers as have left Widows or Issue.
Alphabetical List of the Surnames of all the Peers.

The Archbishops and Bishops of England, Ireland, and the Colonies.
The Baronetage alphabetically arranged.
Alphabetical List of Surnames assumed by members of Noble Families.
Alphabetical List of the Second Titles of Peers, usually borne by their Eldest Sons.
Alphabetical Index to the Daughters of Dukes, Marquises, and Earls, who, having married Commoners, retain the title of Lady before their own Christian and their Husband's Surnames.
Alphabetical Index to the Daughters of Viscounts and Barons, who, having married Commoners, are styled Honourable Mrs.; and, in case of the husband being a Baronet or Knight, Honourable Lady.
Mottoes alphabetically arranged and translated.

"Lodge's Peerage must supersede all other works of the kind, for two reasons: first, it is on a better plan; and secondly, it is better executed. We can safely pronounce it to be the readiest, the most useful, and exactest of modern works on the subject."—*Spectator.*
"A work which corrects all errors of former works. It is a most useful publication."—*Times.*
"A work of great value. It is the most faithful record we possess of the aristocracy of the day."—*Post.*
"The best existing, and, we believe, the best possible peerage. It is the standard authority on the subject."—*Herald.*

RECOLLECTIONS OF

THE LAST FOUR POPES.

BY HIS EMINENCE CARDINAL WISEMAN.

Opinions of the Press.

" A picturesque book on Rome and its Ecclesiastical Sovereigns by
an eloquent Roman Catholic.   Cardinal Wiseman has here treated a
special subject with so much generality and geniality that his Recollections will excite no ill-feeling in those who are most conscien-
tiously opposed to every idea of human infallibility represented by Papal
domination."—*Athenæum.*

" These delightful pages are a record of the favourite impressions
received by the author from scenes, persons, and events, interesting to
all, but pre-eminently so to Catholics."—*Tablet.*

" Among the glories of Rome, these Recollections are not the least."
—*Dublin Review.*

" Messrs. Hurst and Blackett have done good service by publishing a
newly revised and cheaper edition of His Eminence Cardinal Wiseman's 'Recollections of the last Four Popes.'   Such a proceeding suffi-
ciently attests the popularity of this production of the illustrious writer.
This historical work is of peculiar interest to English speaking Catholics, as containing much important information which could proceed
from no other pen.   It is now within the reach of nearly all classes, and
although cheap in the ordinary meaning of the term, it is got up in a
style that reflects the highest credit upon the publishers.   The portraits are especially good, and this new edition may be considered particularly suitable for a Gift Book."—*Weekly Register.*

" This is a new and revised edition of a work upon which criticism
has already pronounced its judgment.   The accomplished author never
fails to invest with interest any subject on which he writes or speaks.
It is no wonder, then, that this book should have commanded the
attention and, in many respects elicited the approval, of even those
who most widely differ with him in his views of the Pontificate, and of
the administrative institutions of modern Rome.   The new edition of
the 'Recollections' is published at, even for this age of cheap literature, the remarkably moderate price of 5s.; though it is a good-sized
volume, beautifully printed, and illustrated."—*Sun.*

" Biography is one of the most interesting departments of literature,
but it is peculiarly so when derived from personal knowledge, and based
on observation.   The present work, on account both of its subject and
its author, is a literary curiosity, and certainly the expectations which
may be formed of it will not be disappointed.   Cardinal Wiseman is
one of the most eminent dignitaries of the Roman Church, and as such
is sure to command a wide audience; but he is also one of the first
scholars and ablest writers of the day.   In the present work he has
kept aloof from controversy; and it must be admitted that on the whole
he writes in a free and tolerant spirit.   His sketches of Vatican life
might have been penned by Benvenuto Cellini, they are so candid and
at the same time so graphic.   He has done wisely to write his work
for all creeds, and it may be read by all with equal profit and interest."
—*United Service Magazine.*

HURST AND BLACKETT, PUBLISHERS, 13, GREAT MARLBOROUGH STREET.